THE STARTING BLOCK

By Robert McCutcheon

Bellissima Publishing
Jamul, California

This book is historical fiction. Any resemblance to actual persons living or dead is purely coincidental.

Copyright © 2006 by Robert McCutcheon

All rights reserved. No part of this book may be reproduced or transmitted in any means whether mechanical, electronic or photocopying or recording, or any information storage and retrieval system without express written permission from the publisher and author.

Published by Bellissima Publishing, LLC, Jamul, California
www.bellissimapublishing.com

Printed in the United States of America

ISBN 0-9776993-8-2
First Edition

For My Parents

THE STARTING BLOCK

By Robert McCutcheon

The Starting Block

CHAPTER ONE

My Brother Sort of Wins

On a Saturday afternoon in early March, Billy and I sat in the bleachers of Trees Pool and watched my brother Chip win the 400-yard freestyle in the 1967 Western Pennsylvania Interscholastic Athletic League championships.

The realization that the swimmer whom the crowd (which included yourself) was cheering as the victor was also your brother was a remarkable one, especially considering that he lost.

I loved being in the pool, but I loved this spot, too. Billy and I had found seats away from everyone else, high in the bleachers, almost under the concrete eaves of the huge, Olympic-sized natatorium on the campus of the University of Pittsburgh. The water seemed far below, like an oblong, sapphire-blue crater lake. The diving platforms rose on our left, a ten-meter mountain range. Through the floor-to-ceiling windows behind them, under weak late-winter sunlight, that landscape of cement extended into the city streets of Oakland. Some cindery snow, as dingy as the asphalt, still crusted the curbs. I was with all that on the outside. With Chip swimming, though, it was almost as though I was in the pool at the same time that I was watching it from above.

Once the starter's gun had cracked for the start of the 400 and the swimmers knifed into the water, a cavernous silence settled over the pool. The sole sound was the rustle of their strokes, the slapping feet of flip turns. It was the longest race on the program, sixteen lengths of the pool, and the spectators settled in and waited for the field to take shape. There were a few cheers, but in the chlorinated breeze they seemed unconnected to the race, maybe even trapped up in the rafters, like errant birds, left over from earlier races. From the last row, I could imagine that I was the only one watching, or seeing what was actually happening.

"Look," Billy said. "The Scull is back."

He was right. He was in lane two.

Billy and I enjoyed classifying the various species of freestyle. This swimmer from an alien high school had earned his name the previous year at this same meet. He had one of the more distinctive strokes on display: after a nearly straight-armed, surface-skimming recovery, his hands entered the water cupped outward, as if he was pulling to the side, each arm like the oar of a single scull—though underwater he was no doubt executing a standard S-stroke. He was good. The Flywheel was back, too. This guy had a herky-jerky stroke, one hand always thrashing to catch up to the other as he turned his head to breathe. He looked as though he was struggling toward a lifeboat. But he was good, too. Everyone in the finals was fast. Chip by contrast had a textbook stroke. In fact, he had learned it from a textbook, which I was used to seeing propped open all over the house.

It was possible these weren't the same guys as last season. The swimmers changed; the strokes were eternal. But one of them was the same.

Progar was Chip's archrival, from Penn Hills. He met him once or twice a summer and a couple of times during the year and had yet to beat him.

"Ah, there's no call for that."

This remark came from the man in the row in front of us. Heavy-set and quiet to this point, he was tapping his program against the palm of one hand

It was late in a race that had turned out just the way we expected, or dreaded, with Progar pulling slowly away from the rest of the field. His lead was about as incremental as you could want. For the first few lengths he turned only slightly ahead of everyone else, but always a little less slightly, and soon there was clear water and a three-count before the nearest guy, who was not Chip, turned after him.

The Starting Block

His last turn was different; that's what had prompted the man's comment. Progar's counter yelled "Fifteen!" and folded up his set of plastic numbers. But then, after his push-off, Progar flipped onto his back and lifted his head so he could watch the competitors in his wake. He was also a good backstroker.

"Come on," the man said, not quite to himself. "Why hot dog it? You won the race."

An adult below him, though he acted amused, seemed to take mild exception to this remark. He looked up and shrugged. "Hey, it's freestyle, pal." In jeans and a jacket with *Penn Hills* stenciled on the back, he was dressed for a high school football game, except for the stopwatch in his left hand. "Do whatever stroke you want."

Chip finished with two or three others in a flurry.

"He got second," I said to Billy. "He out-touched the Scull."

We waited as the others finished and climbed out, more or less dogged in defeat. We were watching Chip shake the water off and then keep shaking his head in apology, or resignation, or disappointment as he walked over toward the stands when we realized something strange was taking place on the deck of the pool.

"Is Progar celebrating?" Billy asked.

"Nice celebration," the man below us said; and all of a sudden we were talking to him.

The Starting Block

If it was a celebration, it took a strange form. Progar wasn't exactly dancing, though you could take it for that. He was pacing up and down, gesticulating with his towel, the way kids snap them in locker rooms.

Progar's name disappeared from the electronic scoreboard. It was replaced with "Livingstone, C.," and a fresh ovation went up.

"Chip won?" I asked, surprised at the development.

The ruling worked its way up to us from the pool deck. Our new friend explained it to us. The man in the Penn Hills jacket had somehow in the confusion gotten himself onto the pool deck, where he was talking to the starter.

"True, you can swim any stroke you want in freestyle," the man explained, as though he had drafted the rule. "But you can't switch from one to the other in a race. If you start with freestyle, you'd better stick with it. You can't make up your very own individual medley. That will get you disqualified every time."

"Look at the way Mom and Dad are waving," Billy said. "He *must* have won."

While the announcement was being made, down in the first row, our parents, as naturally as they could, were trying to make the transition from consoling Chip to congratulating him and at the same time to include us in the celebration.

The Starting Block

We waved back. Billy was also my brother.

CHAPTER TWO

I Ghost Write My Life

Early in the summer of 1967, after my sophomore year in high school, I began to narrate my own life. It was rather flattering to wake up every morning announced. Even if it was by me.

Teddy Livingstone stirred uneasily from his sleep, at once intrigued and disappointed to discover that for some time he had been lying face down in a pool of saliva at room, rather than body, temperature. Refocused, his glance fell on the adjacent bed, where his elder brother, Billy, was demonstrating the stage of life Ted himself would occupy before long. That prospect was no more attractive than his sodden pillow: an upper lip peppered with hairs, a pelvis straining against a taut sheet, eyelids rippling with REM. Teddy scissored his legs in sudden assent to consciousness.

The major appeal of this technique was that it put every event immediately into the past tense. Once it was engaged, nothing could happen, exactly. It had happened. The present became redundant. I had just the year before learned of the third-person point-of-view in English class, and I recognized immediately that it was a good way not just to compose a story but to live a life.

Furthermore, I was the third person: the youngest of three brothers evenly spaced at year-and-a-half intervals. We were less evenly distributed around our ranch house in suburban Pittsburgh. Billy and I shared a bedroom, while Chip, the oldest son, had a room to himself farther down the hall I had just entered on my way to learn how this bright Saturday in June would unfold. I had not yet devised a method of narration that would eliminate the future.

Teddy Livingstone stepped barefoot onto the linoleum of the kitchen floor. There was nothing striking about him physically; both his demeanor, on the furtive side though he was in his own house, and the shallow concavity of his posture seemed to indicate his awareness of that fact. If pressed, however, he might concede that he was not bad looking.

His oldest brother, Chip, bellied up to the kitchen counter, would not press him. Teddy obviously expected to be greeted with affectionate derision by Chip, and he was; whereas Billy would later be greeted by derisive derision.

The Starting Block

"Teddy Livingstone is off the block," Chip said, and chuckled.

Ted assumed his drowsy snort would be interpreted as amusement rather than the contempt that that witticism or any other deserved first thing in the morning. But he was used to making allowances for the occasional lapse in his brother's sense of humor, for two related reasons. First, Chip was a swimmer. Second, Ted idolized him.

With the butt of a spoon, Chip was prying open a cardboard drum that contained his protein supplement, a white powder that he would stir into a glass of milk. After one taste I had identified it as bauxite. Maybe swimmers needed their minimum daily amount of aluminum. True, Chip hadn't rusted, despite the hours he spent immersed in water; but it seemed a high price to pay. On the other hand, he had turned a little sanctimonious over the last year or so, not that he didn't have good reason. He had been getting up around 5:30 every morning and was in the pool at six. By nine he was home and monopolizing the kitchen.

He had also turned into the typical, tanned swimmer. A month into the summer his hair was two-toned, blonde and more blonde. His front bang, plastered across his forehead, was bleached like the wood panel on the side of a station wagon. I think they call it wood blonde—sandalwood, ash blonde, or something—and I could see why.

When he came home with his hair slicked back and streaked it looked like a crest carved on the back of a chair. As he drained his glass of sludge his tee shirt rode up, revealing stomach muscles like rungs of a ladder. Underneath his cut-off levis the knot of the drawstring of his tank suit was as white as exposed bone. His navel, surprisingly high up on his stomach, seemed about to snap flat like a wrinkle out of a sheet. A lot of fifteen to seventeen-year-old female age-groupers would have paid good money for that view.

Chip slammed the glass down with a sigh, though he pulled up short and spared Teddy the crack of glass on Formica. Ted's temples pulsed once in anticipation and once in relief. An aspect of Chip's self-righteousness was to indulge in loud post-practice noises.

"Ten threes on four-and-a-half, Teddy," Chip said.

"Wow."

Ted knew he should be impressed, just not how impressed. The appearance of his father, Charles Livingstone, Sr., relieved him of any further reaction. The scent of singed coffee in the air told Ted his parents had had their breakfast.

"Hi, men," Mr. Livingstone said. "And I use the term loosely."

He grabbed his sons by the waistbands of their respective trousers and tugged. Ted surmised there was a wholesomely obscene joke buried deep in the gesture—loose shorts, not too well hung, something along those lines—and hoped another snort would cover it.

"Nice day," Dad said. He directed this remark I felt slightly more into my quadrant of the kitchen than Chip's. "Got plans?"

No, Ted thought; but your cuffless khakis and pocketed blue tee shirt announce that you do.

"Rebuilding a stone wall is a job," Dad said.

Ted had learned over the years to wait his father out. Biting on his first move could result in some household duty. Mr. Livingstone believed deeply in the importance of chores on the one hand but on the other found it impossible to give a direct order. One summer he had drawn up an elaborate work schedule for everyone in the family— cutting grass, washing the cars—then taped it inside the door of his tool shed. Ted had come across it early the next December as they were putting up their Christmas tree.

"It's the little jobs that get you. The ones that need done every week. No energy left for the big ones."

"I told Hooty Hurwitz I'd meet him at the pool," I said, just touching Chip out.

"It was a tough work out this morning," Chip said.

"You rest." Dad wheeled on Chip, suddenly decisive. "You've got another workout this afternoon."

"Coach gave us the afternoon off."

"So you could rest," Dad nodded. "When you don't work out is as important as when you do. And Teddy has a date."

"Not a date, Dad. It's with Hooty Hurwitz."

"Where's Billy?" Dad asked..

"Still asleep," I said.

"What's he doing asleep?"

"Should I wake him up?"

"It's going on ten o'clock."

"Do you want me to get him?"

"To be honest, I don't see how you could live with yourself, sleeping through such a nice day."

"I'll get him," I said, heading back down the hall.

"What did you hold those three-hundreds on, Chip?" Dad said.

As he left the kitchen, Teddy noted with a backward glance that somehow the expression on Mr. Livingstone's face combined concern and glee.

CHAPTER THREE

I Wonder Who Will Help My Father

It occurred to Teddy as he reentered his bedroom that he admired his brother Billy when he was asleep almost as much as he did his brother Chip when he was awake, though for different reasons. Billy was the most uninhibited sleeper he had ever seen. When he was comatose he made no effort to conceal the fact. He was in a different but equally fervent position when Teddy returned, head craned back, palms up as though midway through a religious experience, which for him sleep probably was, more so at least than going to church.

"Billy."

Ted sat down on his bed and waited.

"Das-das. Zim bil?"

It was the speaking in tongues that had given Ted his first clue as to the religious nature of sleeping for Billy.

He waited longer.

"It's gone," Billy said, reverting to his native English. "I know it's gone. There are too many boxcars, you know?"

"I know," I said.

"They looked."

"I know."

"What?" Billy said, his eyes suddenly clear.

"Never mind," I said. "Dad wants you."

As he and his brother Chip started down the path to the pool, Teddy Livingstone looked back in the direction of his house, back into the sun and the drone of a two-stroke gasoline engine, to see Billy mowing the horizon.

CHAPTER FOUR

I Report to the Pool

"Oh, hi, Hoot."

If he tried, Teddy could not have exaggerated the offhandedness of Ed Gow's salutation. As Hooty edged through the door into the guards' room, Ed twisted in his chair, spoke, then turned erectly yet effortlessly back to the paperwork on the desk in front of him.

"Hi," Hooty said. Then, as he closed the door on the phosphorescent day outside he said, "Sorry."

The rest of us winced and nodded. Ed's pre-emptive greeting had wrung all the camaraderie out of the cinder-block lifeguards' lounge at the rear of Community Swim Club. Only Gow would have called him "Hoot." "Hooty" was a ridiculous enough nickname to start with, after all.

"Horny as a hoot-owl," J. T. Orum remarked, without much conviction.

"What's up?" Hooty singled me out and sat down on the crusty arm of the sofa.

Teddy couldn't help but feel that Ed had tried to make the greeting sound like an insight, as though maybe no one else would have thought to say hello.

"I forgot it was such a good year," Chip said. He sat on the matching armchair, overstuffed and faded, leafing through a tattered holiday issue of *Playboy*—one of the fat ones, probably January. J. T. was just down from the chair. His zinced-up nose glowed like a night-light through the gloom.

What it was, Teddy thought, was Ed's contribution to see Hooty first. Then he could sit there for the rest of the day. He was the kind of guy who liked to drive. All he asked was to have a clearly defined role in a given group. Like ordering paper cups.

"Hoops?" I asked.

Hooty shrugged.

Underneath us, the humming pumps shifted like gears.

It wasn't that Ed hadn't done it with a certain style.

Chip was off that afternoon. As his brother and presumptive member of the staff next year, I had loitering privileges in the guards' room. Hooty gained entry as my friend, and I knew I could count on him to be properly deferential in my future workplace.

When a reality was as obvious as the one in that room—i. e., that Ed was an essential yet at the same time barely tolerated member of the group—Teddy couldn't see why it was not openly acknowledged. And if it couldn't be, no wonder still greater realities weren't.

"Who got Playmate of the Year?" Chip asked. "If it wasn't Miss May I demand a recount."

"Miss November," Ed said without looking up.

CHAPTER FIVE

We Reconnoiter

From his deck chair on the terrace, T. A. L. surveyed the scene of festive devastation in front of him. People writhed in the pool like ants stuck in syrup. Bodies lay all over the grass, smitten by the sun. Meanwhile, Teddy had never in his life felt so utterly in control. He and Hooty had grabbed the corner table, right in the traffic flow to the snack bar and the dressing rooms, so that everyone had to pass their slitted gaze on their way to the water.

Everyone.

"Maybe her family's away on vacation," Hooty said.

"They go in August, someone told me."

The girls were all wearing two-pieces that summer, a development that Theo applauded. Some of the new fabrics were outstanding.

"You're right. I think that's her sister."

"Where?"

Hooty pointed toward the tennis court, where a couple of very young girls were engaged in activity more like volleyball. The older sister in question was a girl named Cindy Flood who had moved into the school district midway through the year and very shortly thereafter into Teddy's fantasy life. He had been both pleased and petrified to learn that her family had joined Community Swim Club, of which his own family was a founding member and in whose employ his brother Chip currently was. Teddy had yet to speak to her in any venue.

There was a second state of affairs around the swimming pool that T. L. found staggering in its transparency, in both senses of the word. Were or were not women in bathing suits naked? Even in the one-piece tank suits the girls on the team wore to practice and occasionally socially as well. Ignore the extremities and you had a nylon pod that contained sex. Everyone female in the club carried around her sex pod and pretended she didn't.

In the space of time it took Hooty to shift in his chair from hip to the other, Cindy was by them, with her mother and a cooler running interference.

While no actual exchange had taken place between Cindy and Teddy, there could be little doubt that some communication had.

The Starting Block

Otherwise Cindy would not have turned her head that way when she and her mother reached the deep end deck. She would hardly have glanced off toward the woods except to imply a void in her life that young Livingstone could a) understand and b) fill.

Some things were, after all, necessarily better left unsaid.

"Hoops?" Hooty asked.

It was true that the basketball court had come free.

I shrugged.

CHAPTER SIX

I Assist My Brother

"Make sure you take a shower before you go in the pool. You're filthy."

Chip's voice floated matter-of-factly over my shoulder, but he was talking to Billy, who must just have arrived. A quick glance up into the glare confirmed that he had. He was trailing his tee shirt from the back of his shorts, but its recent position on his torso was indicated by the collar and long sleeves of grime and glass clippings he still wore.

Billy pulled up a chair. "I just got here. You don't have to shower to walk through the front gate." After a scrape of aluminum on concrete he leaned toward me. "He's not even on duty."

The timing of Chip's riposte told Ted that he had started away and then come back. Teddy *was busy watching his retinas do their surface-of-the-sun imitation.*

"Tomorrow I'm sweeping the pool, and I don't want to find any of your dirt on the bottom," Chip said.

"Nobody ever takes a shower," Billy offered.

For the excellent reason, Teddy *reflected, that the pool management had located the nearest glacier and piped in the run-off for that purpose.*

"Look," Chip said, pulling up another chair, suddenly expansive. "The people here today don't realize I'm not working."

It was hard to know how they could, since Chip was in uniform: sunglasses, blue nylon shorts, and balmy lips.

"It's a rule, and I can't play favorites. You *have* to take a shower. Besides," he repeated, "you're filthy."

"I'm not even going in," Billy said, as sweat trickled alluvially down his arms.

There was a pause for one pulse of the sun.

"Teddy, can you count for me?" Chip said.

"You're not going to swim laps *now,* are you?" I. asked, annoyed.

One of Teddy's chief brotherly duties was to sit at the end of the pool at meets or in practice and flip plastic numbers for Chip while he swam miles on end. Every few lengths he was supposed to hold them under water as Chip turned. But at the moment the pool was seething with kids. Throw in a cow, and you'd pull out a skeleton.

"Not laps," Chip said.

I got up and followed him back to the snack bar. We headed for the parallel bars protruding from the far wall of concrete block.

"Dips?"

Chip shook his head confidentially.

"I'm not going to let Progar beat me on the turns."

He pulled a sit-up board out from behind some stacked chairs and set it at a slant against a rail.

"Here's my problem. I've been swimming long course at the Center in the morning, right? That gives me an edge on Progar. While he's swimming yards over at Chapel Gate, I'm swimming meters. I'm going an extra thirty feet every hundred."

He stopped and put a finger on my sternum.

"But he's doing two more turns per hundred."

Sean Progar was the name of Chip's summertime arch-rival, and Chapel Gate was the name of the team he swam for, the nearest club to us and hence our collective arch-rival. The two meets we swam against them annually as part of the summer league schedule, home and away, were coming up.

Chip turned back and wedged one of his feet under the strap. "So now I've got to do two sit-ups for every hundred I did this morning in practice. I'll do sets of forty, with a minute rest between sets. Like thousands."

He looked around furtively once more before he lowered himself into position. He had nothing to worry about, unless that kid staring at us had a microphone in his popsicle.

Ted felt reasonably sycophantic as he sat there recording his brother's grunts. When he eased off and started counting by tens Chip grunted louder, until Teddy went back to rattling off each repetition. But he recognized through his boredom that he wouldn't have wanted anyone else to have the job. It offered one great advantage: ready conversational matter.

When I lifted my head, Cindy was looking me right in the eye from the snack bar.

"Hi," she said.

"Thirty-four, thirty-five," I said. "Thirty-six."

When I got back to the table, Hooty was gone and Billy sat in his chair, dripping wet.

Unless Ted missed his guess, the water that cascaded off his brother Billy was chlorinated.

CHAPTER SEVEN

I Watch My Brother Swim

The first sunny Saturday of the season was a lifeguard's showcase. All the stars came out.

By early afternoon the club was jammed like a bazaar. Girls milled around in beach-towel sarongs. Squat women in their skirted, sheet metal bathing suits trailed a kid in each hand. Blankets were spread all over the grass, the deck. People seemed about to break out trinkets and start bartering.

A week ago we were in school.

I could tell every time Chip passed behind us because of the kids tailing him saying, "Are you going *in*, Chip? Are *you* going in?"

Teddy could never figure out why it was so important to little kids that the guards actually enter the water. He would concede however that for whatever reason this added to a holiday atmosphere.

The Starting Block

As it turned out, Mr. Caldwell, the manager, was the first celebrity to approach the pool. He lumbered out of his plywood office for the two o'clock adult swim. During the year he was a chemistry teacher at the high school, now exposed by streaming sunlight for the sham and hoax it was. As he made his way along the deck in his cap, terry cloth jacket and the khaki trunks that bisected his hirsute, spherical torso, he looked like a big game hunter. In the water he looked like big game. You expected him to wade into the deep end up to his eyes.

Sooner or later Ed Gow would oblige the groundlings. He got down from the chair and, instead of heading back to the guards' room, set his sunglasses, whistle and visor on the low wall by the hedges.

"Ed's going in," kids yelled.

Husbands nudged their wives. Any guard would do.

Ed Gow carried the aspirations of an Olympic diver in the body of a pulling guard. He had the same routine from one summer to the next. He would saunter over to the high dive but then swing arm over arm up the ladder like an enraged primate. Standing toward the back of the board, he would point a toe to roll the fulcrum back. After a high steel worker's walk out to the brink, he would build bounce after bounce, each one higher than the last, ridiculously high, high enough for the world's most spectacular dive, then launch himself into a swoon through the air and crumple against the water.

The Starting Block

The crowd would sigh and then laugh.

But when Ed surfaced he was dead serious. Back up on the board; two bounces and a gainer. Next he spun in a wide-kneed tuck he never came out of, boring forehead-first into the water like a meteor.

The debate on the deck over how many revolutions he made was lively.

Then the chant went up.

"Two and a half!" someone yelled.

"Pike!" someone added.

Ed stood erect, arms stiff at his sides, two-thirds of the way back on the board. This was going to be a real dive. He leaned forward from his ankles, then broke into his approach, three steps and a jump, levering the air with his arms. Somehow he folded that cube of a body into a jackknife and spun it up into the air. But even this dive had a touch of the Gow wit. He had sprung off a corner of the board, enough to throw him out slightly to one side, so that at his entry, instead of reaching for the bottom and maximum points, he tucked into a watermelon right in front of J. T.'s chair, dousing his colleague. Ed then did the prudent thing, swimming underwater to the far side of the deep end, where he climbed out like a geyser with a smirk back at J. T. and a dismissive wave to the crowd. He reached for his sunglasses. No encore.

The Starting Block

That was Chip's cue.

Did they think that when the guards dove in they would walk across the water on their hands? That when they jumped they would bounce off the surface like a trampoline?

The eyes of the crowd swiveled as one toward the shallow end. The sea of swimmers parted to make a lane down the middle of the pool. In a single motion Chip had adjusted his goggles and stepped up and off the block into his semiformal racing dive, hands dangling and body in the slightest pike. His feet scraped the water a fraction of a second before his hands hit. His distance-swimmer's stroke was a thing of beauty: elbows high, hands like blades. His kick followed like an escort of dolphins that surfaced at intervals with a splash. He began his turns impossibly far from the wall, it seemed, and flipped them ostentatiously slowly; on the most nonchalant his legs cart wheeled out of the water so that his feet hit the wall one at a time. After his fourth turn he coasted to a stop and stood up in the shallow end. Everyone went back about their business as though they hadn't been paying attention and as though they weren't aware that the day and the summer were prematurely past their prime.

But Teddy kept watching as Chip dropped his head back in the water to slick back his hair, turned dark except for a few stray metallic strands, like the kind he had observed in the fabric of certain couches.

The crowd closed around Chip.

CHAPTER EIGHT

My Brother Sort of Loses

To a practiced eye like young Livingstone's, the signs of impending evening were unmistakable.

Mrs. Sieber rose from her chaise lounge with her leafy bathing cap patted into place. She was heading either to the pool or to a camouflaged anti-aircraft station. Girls patrolled the decks barelegged, the bottoms of their wet bathing suits pasted to the tails of their tee shirts like two stamps. The guard's chair in the deep end was empty. Mr. and Mrs. McDonald arrived with their picnic basket.

Billy came to with a start, nearly coherent.

"What is time?" he asked.

At that moment J. T. stood up in his chair and spared me what could have been a very complicated answer:

"Five o'clock. All children under the age of fourteen not accompanied by an adult must leave the pool at this time."

The sun's rays came at us head-on, like a wind.

It was bad form to leave the club right at five o'clock with the kids; however, our group swagger should have set Billy, Hooty and me apart as we exited the front gate. We went home through the woods behind the shopping center along the path that followed the creek and fed into the old baseball field as though into a grassy lake.

Ted thought at first it was an apparition. Then he hoped it was. But apparitions didn't wear St. Christopher medals, and they weren't escorted by Donnelly and Scott.

We stutter-stepped like a chorus line.

"Little Liv." Progar accosted Billy, who was in the lead. "Where's your *big* brother?"

Ted hadn't thought Progar either noticed him or, if he did, knew who he was; but this emphasis seemed a veiled allusion to his existence.

"Me and him have some unfinished business."

It surprised Ted that he was aware of Billy's existence, for that matter.

Donnelly and Scott almost smirked.

Like the nation at large, our suburb had two of everything. Just as there was Coke and Pepsi, Heinz and Campbell, Lestoil and Mr. Clean—all identical—so there was Community Swim Club and Chapel Gate Swim Club. Again, Progar was Chapel Gate's top swimmer,

Chip's swarthy counterpart. But you might take him for a weight lifter; his arms and chest were copper-plated with muscle. In the glare of the sun his short, curly black hair looked like lace against his scalp.

It wasn't the menace of a situation like this that got to Teddy. As always, it was the unspoken. It seemed to Ted that everyone present was aware of and faintly pleased by his participation in this time-honored ritual, as though one of them might say, "I am aware of and faintly pleased by my participation in this time-honored ritual: Older Tough Guy Confronts Younger Brother of Arch-Rival." Progar was savoring the lead role with a sneer.

No one said anything for a minute.

Donnelly belched. Then he said, "Spread out."

Teddy wished, after all, that he had taken a minute before they left the pool to visit the men's room.

"Don't he walk you home?" Progar asked with a sneer.

Teddy supposed Progar's remarks didn't call for a reply, but he still wished that Billy would say something. Or, if not, that he wouldn't look as though he was trying to think of something to say.

"He's a lifeguard at Community, isn't he?" Progar said. "Only, he don't seem to be guarding your life."

Donnelly reached into the breast pocket of his shirt for his cigarettes. He shook one out of the pack and offered it to Scott. For some reason Donnelly was wearing a blue, button-down, Oxford-cloth dress shirt over khaki slacks. These private-school kids never really learned how to relax; besides, that is, from hanging out with public school thugs. At least his shirttails were out. And there were no socks under his penny loafers. With his doughy, droopy face, Donnely bore some resemblance to Popeye, right down to his impressive forearms, which looked to be the only developed muscle on an otherwise puffy body. Scott was a big, broad-beamed kid with precocious sideburns. The pockets on the back of his levis were window-sized. He had been held back in the second or third grade; he'd had the sideburns then, too.

Any sign of boredom from these two guys would be hopeful, but they seemed to be settled in for an enjoyable smoke.

Try as he might, Ted could not remember the last time he had urinated.

"I understand your brother is getting up early these days. I saw him driving home once about nine. What ever do you think he's doing?"

"He's swimming," Billy said dryly.

"Can you be more . . . 'specific?'" Progar eased the polysyllable into the conversation, but not past Donnelly and Scott, who raised another smirk. "What kind of sets is he doing?" he asked, and for the moment he seemed genuinely interested.

"I'm not sure," Billy shrugged. "Quantity stuff, I think. Low rest."

The Starting Block

Donnelly farted. Progar seemed to accept that statement as self-explanatory, though Scott said, "Cut it off so it don't trail."

Ted remained firm in his conviction that, far from feeling antagonism, all present were simply deepening the bond among them. He fully expected someone, perhaps it would be Scott, to say, beaming, "We've done it, lads! Haven't we just acted out a universal adolescent ritual? Bravo!"

"What about you, little, little Liv the second? Does he discuss his workouts with you?"

"He don't say what he does."

That was less than the truth, but Ted felt he was being conciliatory, as well as playing his part in the ritual, by letting his grammar deteriorate.

"You probably know he so-called beat me in the four hundred at WPIALs. You was both probably there."

On the other hand, Ted knew full well that the time-honored Older Tough Guy Meets Younger Brother of Arch-Rival scenario could develop into the equally time-honored Older Tough Guy Beats Younger Brother of Arch-Rival to a Pulp scenario.

Scott dropped his cigarette half-smoked in sudden distaste.

I figured that if I had to hit Donnelly, one of two unpleasant things would happen, aside from ultimately getting beat up. Either his face would collapse around my fist like risen dough or the force of my blow would prompt some bodily eruption from him. Possibly both.

"You heard the Chapel Gate cheer?" Progar asked; but his question was really a statement.

Billy shook his head.

I was the only one who saw Chip. He was off on our right, and Progar's left, on a parallel path. The way the light glinted off his hair he seemed to be in the center of a clearing that moved along with him. I felt rooted in the middle of the trail like any sapling. If I opened my mouth to call him, a leaf would come out.

Although Teddy could not move, his bladder dropped a notch.

I watched as Chip's hair flickered and finally faded into the shadows under our hill. The experience made me look forward to my next nightmare. At the same time, I wasn't sure I would have wanted Chip to enter this scene. Although he was my older, stronger and bigger brother, I couldn't imagine him in a fight.

Donnelly farted again, this time with the effect of ripped fabric. Perhaps fabric *had* ripped.

Progar spread his arms and smiled, as though they had overlooked the obvious and said, "The cheer is, 'Beat you in the meet or beat you in the street.'"

Behind me a twig snapped like the report of a starter's pistol, but the tone of the remark that followed was not menacing. Rather, unlike anything that had been said so far, it was reasonable, even kindly.

"A path through the woods is not a street," Chip said, breaking through underbrush, "unless you're using the term in a *very* loose sense. A cheer is meant to be inspirational, but it should *still* be specific."

The moment most dreaded and yet most longed for by Ted in such a confrontation had arrived, the moment of its maximum transparency, when tedium, ill will and sincerity all hung in an awful balance. Progar's pecs tensed; for a split second his nipples pointed straight at the ground. With an amputee's reflex Scott glanced down at his hand for the absent cigarette. No one thought of anything to say. In a brief vision Ted watched his bladder bounce down the trail like a beach ball. The next movement could just as easily be a left hook as a pleasantry—the latter, if Ted's fellow teen-agers read the ritual aright. They had already demonstrated, at least to Ted's satisfaction, that they shared their generation's ideal of surly, surfeited adolescence.

After a minute Donnelly lobbed an observation over Progar's shoulder and said, "Cawley's waiting at the shopping center."

"Is he out on parole already?" Chip asked.

Donnelly winced at Chip's remark, but Scott expelled a hiss of laughter. Progar looked thoughtful.

Then Chip spoke again, in my direction. "You look restless, Teddy.   Uncomfortable.   Are we keeping you from some appointment?"

"I got to whiz," I said.

"You *got* to *whiz*?" Chip was pained. "Well, I got here too late. You're talking like these guys."

That was the comment that did it, or its conjunction with Chip's earlier remark, which had implied a common acquaintance in the absent Keith Cawley, another suburban street tough. Scott released a second burst of pressurized amusement. Progar tossed his head in lieu of laughter.

Considering myself excused, I walked up the bank behind us. With each tree I passed, another green veil fell between me and the tableau I had just formed part of. I could still hear them talk—someone even laughed—until I unzipped my fly and watered a patch of glossy weeds and the rush of relief stopped my ears. Now that I was alone and unobserved, any number of bodily functions understandably jostled for my attention. But I didn't expect to have to bend sharply at the waist to tuck myself back into my pants. I left my tee shirt out for good measure.

And, walking back down the slope, ascertaining through the leaves the Progar and his entourage had left, Teddy felt massive relief. He had forgotten that people found it impossible to dislike his oldest brother. They could envy and/or emulate him, but not hate him. Not even Progar, his aquatic alter ego, could hate him. Chip's appearance alone, alert and introspective at the same time, had sufficed to dispel the ill will below. His choice of the word "specific" had been a typical stroke of intuition; he couldn't possibly have overheard Progar use it. In retrospect, Ted saw that his inexplicable arousal relieved itself in a blurted remark of such stupidity that he would be ashamed of it long into the future. The grin with which he reemerged from the woods, turned somehow on himself, still occasionally raked across his memory like the glare of headlights.

"Boy," I said to Chip, returning with springy stride. "Are we glad to see you."

But now Chip seemed distracted. I guess he had been saying something. He looked back at Billy.

"Were you trying to impress someone?" he asked.

Still all but speechless with relief, Ted was unprepared to step forward and remind the lads that the ritual was over. To say to Billy, "You need no longer look down and paw the ground." Or, to Hooty, "Let's don't stand around mute like Donnely and Scott, lest cigarettes sprout from our lips."

"I told you, everyone is supposed to take a shower," Chip said.

Chip didn't exactly beat Billy up. What happened was too businesslike for that. He got his younger brother in some kind of modified headlock—more like a bodylock, if there was such a thing—cradling him with his arms and hip. One second Billy was twisted upside-down on the ground in Chip's grasp and the next he was upright again. It was like one of those jerky sequences in picture books you riffle through. Billy looked different afterward, but you couldn't really tell in what way. Maybe his shirt was on inside out. His expression was quizzical, as though Chip had just made him an intriguing but unprecedented proposal. He would have to think it over and report back.

Chip turned to me. "I told you Progar's out to get me. But if you run into him again, remember, he can be reasoned with."

Teddy must have smiled, because Chip said, "I'm serious." Then he turned back into the woods toward home, and shadow doused his hair.

CHAPTER NINE

I Interview My Brother

Billy isn't that easy to talk to. Maybe because we had always shared a room, we never seemed to start a conversation. It was more as though we had been conducting a fifteen yearlong clarification of some earlier, or rather primordial, conversation.

"Who drove you guys to the dance?" Billy might ask over his shoulder as he sat down on his bed to take his socks off. "Hooty's father?"

"Yeah," I might answer. Or, alternatively, "No."

"Oh," Billy would say. "We decided not to go."

"We" denoted Billy and his girlfriend, Debbie.

"Mr. Marshall drove."

"Oh. Mr. Marshall drove?"

"Yeah."

With that understanding, we would turn off the light.

Maybe Billy thought I hadn't noticed when he passed puberty, a matter of months before I did. Once in a while I would walk into our room just as my brother collapsed the sheet-tent he had stretched over the poles of his knees and assumed the expression of distant annoyance of the onanist caught *in flagrante delicto*. Actually, there was an onanist in the bed next to him, but Billy was the one who always got caught.

That night when I entered the room Billy was lying down fully-clothed on his bed on top of the covers, looking as unimpeachable as possible, probably accumulating innocence against his next exposure. Since I had found him both conscious and uncompromised, I did something dramatic.

I sat down on my bed across from him and asked him a simple question.

You might think that a bedroom shared by two people would be doubly revealing. In fact, it would be hard to find a room with less personality than ours. We kept the family set of encyclopedias in our room, but unless the gold trim of these volumes was mildly radioactive, they had not been absorbed by Billy and me. The yearbook supplements piled up relentlessly; the last decade was in mint condition. Maybe it had not happened yet. While the World Books took up most of the shelf space, the rest was claimed by decommissioned kids' books from all branches of the extended Livingstone family. Our generation had been there at every major battle of World War II, kept a diary at Guadalcanal and flown the Hump—a potential sore spot around the house, since Dad was in western Pennsylvania at the time. On one wall hung a portrait of a deceased baseball player from the wrong league; on another an old b-b gun was mounted over a portrait of Dwight D. Eisenhower. One of us must have expressed an admiration for him during his term of office. You had to be careful: enthusiasms could become permanent if you aired them around your parents. On the other hand, there was a good chance these *objets d'art* had been Chip's.

"Why don't you hate him?" I said.

Billy looked at me blankly.

"I think I understand why you didn't fight back," I went on. "But you must hate him."

"Who, Chip?" Billy said.

"No, Muhammad Ali."

Billy looked me over clinically to ascertain if I were discussing the noted heavyweight champion.

"Yes, your brother, Chip. Do you hate him?"

"Do you?" Billy had still not produced a facial expression.

"No, but he never does anything bad to me. He protects me.

He beats you up."

"He doesn't beat me *up*."

"It certainly looked like it today."

"It's a matter of definition. One brother doesn't beat another up."

"So it's impossible for Chip to beat you up? Even if he tried?"

"That's right. Progar would have beat me up."

"If Chip hadn't arrived."

"Right. Anyway, sometimes I deserve it."

"Not today."

"I don't mean deserve it." A cloud passed across Billy's face as he corrected himself, "Bring it on. This goes back to before you were born."

"You only got here a year before I did."

"Before you were old enough to know what was going on."

I found myself looking at the yearbooks.

"There's another way," I said after a minute.

"What?" Billy asked; and he might have been hailed from across a crowded room.

"Do the opposite of what Progar said. If you can't beat him in the street—if that's logically impossible—beat him in the meet. Beat him in a race."

Billy shook a smile from his face.

"You could do it if you trained harder," I said. "If you

concentrated on the right event. You're bigger than he is. Longer. As soon as you stretch out you're closer to the other end than Chip is. Work on sprints."

"Once I thought I could beat him with Zeno's paradox."

"Come again?" I hadn't expected Billy's bent for mathematics to assert itself just then.

"Zeno was an ancient Greek philosopher who disproved motion."

"Not for long."

Billy collected himself up against the headboard. "Zeno said that as long as a tortoise had a head start over Achilles, Achilles could never overtake it. Because as soon as Achilles caught up to where the tortoise had been, the tortoise would have advanced, even if just a little. I waterproofed that paradox. I figured that as long as Chip and I started out together, and I could prevent him from getting even a fraction of an inch ahead—I mean, if I could keep up with him for just one stroke—he could never beat me to the wall."

"All right," I nodded. "But that just means a tie."

"But I wouldn't lose," Billy said, and paused. "I'll never beat him, Teddy. He's talented. Haven't you watched him?"

We sat and waited.

"About all I could do is pimp him on a relay," Billy said. "False start, something like that. Then he would lose."

"So would you; you're on the relay."

Billy turned his gaze back to me. "You're beginning to grasp the situation. That's the thing about having a brother. You're basically the same person. If you integrate this equation, you conclude that in the long run it's never to your advantage to beat your older brother. You can't win if he loses. Even if you beat him. "

Quivering beneath the deep end of Billy's face I glimpsed the drain of despair.

Ted reflected too late that it would have been wise to narrate this scene.

CHAPTER TEN

I Interview My Other Brother

A more prudent Ted prefaced his narration of his next encounter with the observation that it was only right that the oldest brother should have a bedroom to himself.

Chip's room was at the end of the hall, across from my parents'. They were connected by the master bathroom, which Chip used most of the time, although he staked a claim to ours as well with a can of shaving cream on the windowsill.

I averted my eyes when I walked through the open door onto a scene as embarrassing as any Billy had been guilty of. But Chip didn't seem to think so. He was standing on the far side of his bed with a sock hanging from each hand, bent slightly at the waist, wind milling his arms slowly and humming. He might have been practicing semaphore. When he turned his head to breathe he saw me.

"It helps to visualize," he said, unruffled. He pulled one hand into his stomach, paused, and continued his stroke. "I just made the last turn of the 200 and am heading for home. I like to know what a race looks like beforehand. Also how it comes out. I win." Stabbing for the wall, he straightened up and tossed his socks into his closet. "The event itself will be just a formality."

There was a certain amount of calculated clutter in Chip's room; he was basically a neat person. The most recent issues of *Swimming World* were fanned out on the floor by his bed; the latest *Playboy* was on open display on his nightstand. I knew for a fact that there was a stack of back issues as solid as a tree stump in the corner of his closet. They would not have escaped Mom's scrutiny long in our room. And he did have a lot of books, mostly spongy paperbacks that he devoured and then lined up along the floor under his two brimming shelves. He used trophies as bookends. I could never figure out where he got all the books; in stores, I guess. Maybe there was a family rule I didn't know about that stated the legal ratio of literature to pornography.

I walked in and sat down in the easy chair where he did half of his reading. The rest of the time he lay down on the couch in the living room. About half of that time he remembered to take his shoes off.

"What's on your mind?" Chip said.

"I want to ask you something."

"You mean there is something on your mind? I was just being conversational."

As Ted had suspected, this talk wasn't going to be any easier than the one with Billy. It was the opposite of in the woods. There, in the face of danger, Chip had seemed thoughtful and subdued. Now he couldn't settle down. He seemed elated, carefree; he must just have set a world record for the stationary 200 freestyle.

"Good," Chip went on when I didn't answer. "Because I just learned something about myself: I'm not a sprinter. Naturally I won't be at my best in the summer league, because a hundred is as far as they swim. But that's good for me. If I want to swim a good 500, I'm going to have to swim a good hundred first. People think that you win a distance race with a dramatic kick at the end. No. Well, maybe some tactical race. But to swim your best time you have to keep up a steady speed. Not that you can't pace a hundred. I key on the third length."

A glance over Chip's bed reminded me that he had at one time been a history buff. Painted across the wall in somewhat faded primary colors was a map of the Roman Empire that Chip had worked on, with the blessings of our parents, all through one school year. Numidia was in red. Chip went to sleep every night at the center of the known world. As of A. D. 100, anyway.

"I wanted to talk about Billy," I said.

"Billy," Chip said, dropping his hands and the tee shirt they held to his side. "Billy, I don't think, will ever be a real good swimmer. He's got the build, but not the dedication or the concentration."

"Not about Billy the swimmer... about Billy your brother."

Chip yanked off his jeans and draped them over the chair at his desk. In his underpants, which were more modest than the Speedos in his wardrobe, Chip dove under the sheets on his bed.

"You've got to get things in perspective, Teddy. I personally have a workout early tomorrow morning."

"Why are you so rough on him? Why do you beat him up all the time?"

When he pulled the covers up under his chin and squirmed, he looked more antic than I'd ever seen him, more like a playful uncle than a brother. All that was missing was a nightcap.

"You're not a violent person," I went on. "Competitive, but not violent. You went out of your way to avoid a fight in the woods today. Then you beat up Billy."

"That's my duty," he said. "An older brother is supposed to discipline his younger brother."

"Then you've been remiss," I said.

"How do you mean?"

Chip continued to strike Ted as a little ridiculous as he wriggled his toes under the covers. He was suddenly relieved he hadn't had to witness that performance every night of his life.

"You've never beat me up."

"You're my young*est* brother," Chip said gleefully. When he reached over and turned off his lamp I half expected his eyes to twinkle. "There's a world of difference."

"Then is it Billy's duty to beat me up?"

In the gloom Chip's voice turned dead serious.

"You just let me know if he does."

CHAPTER ELEVEN

A Strange Sabbath

For the first five minutes, the following morning seemed to Ted like a normal Sunday.

The rising tide of sunlight in our room floated me out of bed like a beached boat. Billy was twisted over in my direction, an expression of fierce deliberation on his face. It was always a pleasure to have a path to the closet free of human obstructions, never the case on a school day but always on Sunday, since Billy allowed thirty seconds to get dressed for church. I located my summer suit in the corner where I had hung it the preceding August. It looked fine, marginally less wrinkled for having been jammed between two old overcoats for eight months, but it fit like a shoulder holster. My weightlifting had paid off. Then I reverted to my winter ensemble, a blue blazer and gray sandpaper slacks.

The Starting Block

Dressed for breakfast, Ted entered the kitchen to find his parents sitting at the table in shorts. He was used to being the first kid dressed on Sunday, his only real source of self-righteousness, but invariably Mom and Dad were already fully clothed and in the first stages of panic as ten o'clock approached.

"Why aren't you dressed?" I asked.

"We decided to skip church today," Mom said.

Their calm was unnatural. They passed sections of the newspaper back and forth as though they were playing a card game.

"Why?" I questioned, sounding to myself progressively more parental.

"It's summertime," Mom said, blinking with exaggerated surprise as she looked up suddenly from the paper. "Haven't you noticed?"

The season had never been observed in this way before this.

"Anyway, Chip's still at the pool," Dad said. "They just started Sunday workouts. Practice is later than on weekday mornings. Why should he kill himself?"

"You can eat now if you want," Mom said. "I'll fix lunch later for everyone."

I went back to our room and took off my jacket and pants, which already slid over my skin on a film of sweat, and got into bed. Apparently, Billy had found the answer to the problem he had been wrestling with when I got up, and it wasn't good. He had thrown his head back on the opposite corner of his pillow, appalled.

That was the last Ted heard of church all summer.

CHAPTER TWELVE
Amateur Family Night

Sometime in her early forties my mother decided she should acquire a personality. This seemed in her mind to be one and the same with having a sense of humor. Overnight she became recklessly, irresponsibly upbeat, her overriding object in life to turn the most straightforward occasions into laugh-riots. If Hooty and I were enjoying a quiet game of poker with some other friends, she might enter the room in a visor and sleeve garters carrying a tray of soft drinks, producing a few dry chuckles from my friends and a wince from me. She would break into a teenybopper's twang at the slightest opportunity. She loved to cling to your arm while she laughed at one of the malapropisms that inevitably resulted—she might call your new shirt "base" instead of "boss," which was archaic, anyway—shredding your biceps with her nails as she sank slowly to her knees in mock mortification.

Theodore tried to explain to his mother in private that personality was a liability in parents, and that they had a simple, narrow function to perform. He implored her not to quote top forty songs, still less to sing them, in the course of her daily duties. He would concede that his mother was an attractive woman—but only if she stood still. Any facial expression, but especially a broad laugh at a bad joke, detracted from her appearance.

All that was bad enough. But it occurred to her at about the same time, after fifteen or so years of to me perfectly acceptable child rearing, that the youngest sibling in a family was in danger of being neglected. For the past couple of years I had turned into a soda jerk behind the (ordinarily) vertical counter of my own body. I had every glandular secretion on tap. To apply what I had been learning in school, my physical constitution was much like that of the globe I inhabited. Just as the earth's crust, seemingly so stable, floats on magma, so my skin slid over seas of pus, which might erupt at any moment from any pore. Huge reserves of gas milled around deep in my entrails. And these were only the most mentionable of my natural resources.

My mother developed an uncanny knack of arriving from the remotest quarter of the house immediately on the scene of a bodily function, whether voluntary or involuntary or somewhere in between. I might be peering in a mirror, probing with my fingers the Prudhoe

Bay of my cheeks or the North Slope of my forehead, just as she rounded the nearest corner on the pretext of some household chore. When she came into my room just after an episode of flatulence, all I could do was try to inhale the evidence. Fortunately she didn't smoke; if she lit a match I would be forced to tackle her into the hall outside as my bedroom went up in splinters.

The last thing someone in my state of physical flux wanted was close observation.

One night when Billy was out and Teddy had retired early, his mother entered his room wearing a kindly smile, pulled up a chair beside his bed and said, "It's all right to masturbate." Ted was afraid she meant right then.

It was a matter of public record that she and Dad had had sex three times. My brothers and I were living proof that she was no virgin. On the other hand, there was nothing to suggest that my mother and father had copulated more than three times. Very likely three acts of coitus in the early fifties had ushered in a decade and a half of amicable domestic partnership.

At the same time, I would have liked to see a little physical affection between them. When he left for work in the morning, my father bunched his lips up into a rubber stamp that he aimed at the pad of my mother's right cheek. After dinner I expected them to shake hands and exchange pats on the butt.

Ted admitted to a little ambivalence on the subject of his parents and their relations.

The very fact that Mom seemed to schedule her sessions with me proved that she liked Chip best. She probably thought I suspected and resented that preference. But I didn't. I shared it.

I don't mean to sound completely cynical about our family life that summer. In many ways it was very pleasant. Sometimes it was nearly normal. On the whole, I preferred living in our house to living in someone else's. Sleeping over with a friend was an exhilarating experience until you woke up to discover that his entire family put ketchup on their scrambled eggs. Burrowing into the side of a hill in the woods behind our house was intriguing, which it occurred to me sometimes to do, so that I could lead a solitary life yet still have access to a toaster.

It was in the kitchen that our family appeared in its best light. It seemed a meal was always in progress. We all maneuvered around each other as we made our way from counter to cabinet, something like a water ballet without the water. Chip ate after his morning workouts, spooning an assortment of supplements into a variety of shakes and sludge. Billy, on the other hand, liked to have a quick ham on rye immediately before practice. Ingeniously, he had discovered that by lifting an electric ring on the stovetop and placing his sandwich underneath it he could create an individual grill.

I often felt sorry for my father in this setting. He seemed disoriented, almost dizzy, as we wheeled around him where he stood in the middle of the floor, staring in dismay not only at the quantity of food we put away—"What do you think it is around here, government surplus?" —but at its very existence. He demonstrated a surprising command of brand names. "What was in here," he would ask plaintively, holding up an empty plastic tray. "Vienna Fingers? Did we have Vienna Fingers, Marge?" Or, looking longingly at a bleached skeleton on the kitchen counter, "That chicken was stuffed, wasn't it?" Despite these disappointments, to his credit, he never became bitter. His face still fell every time he opened a half-gallon of ice cream, only to find a small drift in the bottom corner. He would skim a crusty spoonful off an end flap gratefully.

Ironically, some our finest scenes began with Chip's tantrums. He always seemed wound up pretty tight, on account of all his swimming was Dad's theory, and prone to outbursts. But he was so ridiculously sarcastic that his tirades always came out funny. One Saturday morning Mom and I sat alone at the kitchen table when Chip walked in from his workout. Without a word he opened the refrigerator door and immediately dropped his arms to his side in disgust. At the same time, he seemed to expect whatever it was he saw inside.

"All right," he said. "What *swine* drank my Instant Breakfast?"

Mom wrinkled up her nose and said laughing, "Chip. It won't take a minute to mix another glass. After all, it is 'instant' breakfast."

That was a pretty good example. Not "pig," or "hog," but

"swine".

Chip slammed the door of the refrigerator shut, producing more of a 'chunk'.

"I make a point to mix a glass of Instant Breakfast before practice so that it's ready for me when I get back. I still have to put in protein powder. If anyone else around here got their buttocks out of bed at six in the morning, they might understand my point of view. Besides, that was the last one," he said opening the refrigerator and peering inside one more time.

"Oh, no," Mom said. "I feel sure there's more."

"I'm glad you feel that way," Chip said. "That must be a nice feeling to have. Even, or especially, if there is no more. "

He closed the door more gently this time, with an air of insight, and turned toward the table and queried, "Why do you always automatically assume that there's more of something?"

By this time Mom was on her knees on the counter, rummaging through an overhead cabinet. With a flourish, she handed down an unopened box.

"Strawberry," Chip said. "My favorite after-workout flavor," he added as he wheeled and accosted the refrigerator again. "Even if there were more vanilla, that wouldn't alter the fact that there's been a swine loose in here. And furthermore, it was a stupid swine, who mistook that refrigerator for a large, white, upright trough."

Ted couldn't help but be amused at his brother in full flight.

"Oh, Chip," Mom said.

"And I think I know the identity of that swine. Billy!" he yelled, still at the refrigerator, which he apparently considered Billy's accomplice. "Get in here."

"He's not up," I said. "He's the only one who's *not* up."

"He was walking in his sleep again," Chip said. "He drank it and went back to bed."

"Chip," Mom implored.

Chip opened the door once more and spoke directly into the refrigerator, and said, "There's a swine in the house. Now who is he?"

Suddenly Dad appeared in the kitchen. He walked up behind Chip and said, "Oink, oink."

Billy wandered into the room and wanted to know what was so funny.

Every so often these sketches blossomed into a formal event. For some reason, maybe on a Thursday night in early summer, the family would congregate in the living room after dinner. Chip didn't have a book open face down over the arm of his reading chair; Billy hadn't scheduled a call to his girlfriend. Mom and Dad would drift over to the couch with their coffee. There was something eerily natural about these scenes. Everyone seemed to know not to remark on it, or we would scatter like squirrels to every corner of the house.

At that point the Livingstone Brothers went into action. We worked primarily as soloists, appearing in order of age. Chip's forte was impressions of local merchants. He was brilliant; he could have made a career of it if only Larry Wetzel, the stammering grocer, had been a national figure. Recently Chip had taken our car to get fixed by a mechanic with gratuitously bad grammar and incorporated him into his routine. As a backup he had some impersonations of the Kennedy family, actually an imitation of an old record of Kennedy impressions we had acquired at the time.

Billy's routine had an even narrower appeal. After Chip had warmed the audience up, Billy would enter from the hall in one of my father's cardigans and, if the atmosphere was particularly festive, one of my mother's bathing caps to simulate Chuck's dome. As Billy pulled a chair up to an imaginary dinner table and his eyes narrowed to a glint at the prospect of equally imaginary stuffed pork chops in front of him, my father's grin would ratchet a notch or two tighter. When Billy asked for "a trifle more mashed potatoes" he brought down the house.

During all the hilarity Teddy registered the irony that the son who had been wedged unnoticed into the middle of the family was the one who had observed all his parents' quirks.

As an encore, which was always necessary, Billy would do Mom and Dad together. He had a famous rendition of a dialogue that had taken place between them one night on the other side of our bedroom wall. He used exactly the same muffled voice for both of them, which made it all the funnier.

"'Chuck, are we going to go see Roller Derby tomorrow?' . . . 'I don't *want* to go see Roller Derby tomorrow, Marge' . . . 'But, Chuck, you *said* we could go see Roller Derby tomorrow.'"

No one could remember when Roller Derby had come to town, but the conversation itself was plausible.

Teddy provided the evening's musical number. The twist had been his mainstay for years, ever since he had discovered by accident that he could thicken his voice into quite a creditable Chubby Checker. But as he announced himself on that early summer evening, his lungs billowed like the floor-length curtains behind him with the warm breeze of inspiration.

"Ladies and gentlemen," I began. "I know that over the years you have come to expect the latest dance step from me."

"Have you heard of this new 'twist?'" Chip said to laughter.

"But tonight—tonight you can look forward to a departure."

My family responded with their impersonation of a startled courtroom.

"A departure to the familiar, if you will."

Both reassured and intrigued, the crowd settled again.

"Not the latest craze hot off American Bandstand, but an evening of old-fashioned romance. However, I will require the help of my assistants." I snapped my fingers. "William, may I ask you to resume the role for which you have been so widely acclaimed, that of Chuck Livingstone?"

To a thunderous ovation, Billy smoothed the bathing cap back over his head.

"And, in a special guest appearance, Charles Livingstone, Jr., will play the part of Margaret Livingstone."

Chip's expression went blank. Reclining at one end of the couch, he swatted away the renewed applause of the crowd. "I've retired for the evening. Anyway, I'm a soloist."

"Prima donna," Dad joked, giving him a shove on the shoulder.

Chip grimaced. "I don't want to be Mom."

"Go on, Chip," Mom said. "I'm flattered by the thought."

With another groan, Chip hauled himself out of the sofa and collapsed in the chair I had set beside Billy's.

I continued. "Tonight's episode is entitled, 'Chuck and Marge Rekindle Their Romance in the Sixties.'"

"Ooh, how exciting," Mom said, hunching her shoulders and batting her eyelashes.

Uncharacteristically, Teddy had failed to anticipate that his subject would bring out the newfound jocularity of his mother.

I began a medley of songs, opening with "Everybody Loves Somebody Sometime."

Ted's Dean Martin was not bad, either.

"Now, hold hands, Chuck and Marge." Standing between Billy and Chip, I tried to pull their hands together. Chip's arm dragged like a lane rope that had to be stretched into place.

The Starting Block

"Come on, Teddy," he said. "What is this?"

But I addressed the crowd on the couch. "I urge the audience to participate. Act along with the actors." And at that point I went soul with a Sam Cook selection.

As he crooned the crucial lines, "But I know that if you loved me too, what a wonderful world it would be," and his mother and father flapped their arms around each other and puckered up, it occurred to Ted to segue to his imitation of Sam Cook vomiting.

Building to a climax, I broke into my money number, a raucous James Brown song complete with choreographed back-up singing. "*Love* your woman," I screeched. "*Show* her that you care."

When I squeezed Chip and Billy together by the shoulders, the latter stayed in character, cooing the Chuckesque words, "Smooch me, Marge."

"Get off me," Chip said, shoving Billy half off his chair. "And, shut up, Teddy. You're worse than a case of swimmer's ear."

Teddy would be the first to concede that his falsetto could be penetrating at a range of two inches.

When Billy renewed his advances, still laughing, Chip punched him squarely in the deltoid.

"Knock it off, you two," Dad said, starting from the couch.

"Boys," Mom said.

"Now what's Teddy mad about," I heard Dad say.

"Well, his skit is ruined," Mom said.

The Starting Block

By that time I was out the front door. "This family makes a joke out of everything," I yelled back over my shoulder.

From the front yard, I could see everyone else framed like a silent movie in the picture window. Billy stood at the curtains, which he had just drawn back. Chip was gesticulating to Mom and Dad. They might or might not have heard me.

CHAPTER THIRTEEN

A Friend for the Lovelorn

That was the other thing Ted meant to mention: these festivities always ended in acrimony. But he acknowledged that they had to. Otherwise the fun might go on forever. And since it was impossible to predict his family's good moments, or rather exactly when they would turn into excruciating ones, Ted preferred to do his entertaining off the premises, specifically at the Hurwitz residence, his destination in the immediate aftermath of his aborted skit.

Hooty came from the other kind of family. No one in it seemed connected to anyone else. They didn't even look alike. Hooty had an older sister off studying somewhere in Europe and another, much younger sister still in grade school. Where Hooty was lanky and blonde, this sister was small, dark and intense. Her black, wiry hair was always clustered around her head like an electron cloud. Whenever I asked over the phone if Hooty was home she was inclined to answer "Yes" and let it go at that. To judge by the portrait in her college yearbook, Hooty's older sister Elissa was an austere beauty in black and white. Like the picture, her empty bedroom, which we passed on our way down the hall to his, seemed slightly blurred by absence. Both Hooty's parents were professors at the university of subjects I had never heard of; each of them could be addressed optionally as "Dr.". Hooty and I could go into his room and talk without fear of intervention while his sister played in her room and his mother and father read in the den. There was an oriental rug in every room in the house.

It wasn't that we avoided his parents. I approached them at some point in every evening I spent at Hooty's house. Bent over their books, they seemed poised to be interrupted in unison. They were always eager to listen; once they got to discussing a topic they could be hard to get away from. When I broached one of my many complaints about school or social relations, Mr. Hurwitz's reaction, easily misinterpreted, was always the same. He would lift his glasses and drop his book into his lap in disgust, not, as it turned out, at my sniveling, but at the people responsible for it, usually a branch of government. My inability to get ahead in life by cutting grass prompted a tirade against the legislature.

"The boy wants to work," he burst out. "Can't the morons in

Congress see that? Let them work for minimum wage and see how they like it."

I always felt much better with my problems in perspective.

Sex for the elder Hurwitzes, Ted reasoned, would be conducted in the spirit of an advanced jigsaw puzzle. They probably wouldn't take their sweaters off.

Hooty was a serious musician. One night he and I sat on the floor of his room, or rather *he* sat; I lay prone in front of a stack of old *Sports Illustrated*s. Hooty balanced a small electric keyboard on his lap and gazed quizzically from under his headphones into space. After a while he laughed and said, "That's it."

"What?" I asked, looking up from my reading. I had been catching up on the Turkish national wrestling team.

"Listen," he said as he struck the kind of jangling chord you might hear at a crucial moment in a game show. "It's diminished. I should have known that."

I returned to the fine print of the *Sports Illustrated*. Hooty had just exemplified for me once again the best friend: someone who had many admirable but essentially worthless skills. Nothing that could get you in "Faces in the Crowd." An eight- year-old kid had recently swum a record mile—out in California, probably in a pool much like ours and in chemically similar water. A woman had won her fifth straight international skeet-shooting title. These things were worthy of note! I guessed Hooty had a good ear. He would spend hours with a record figuring it out rather than buy the sheet music. First he would study it through the headphones his father had gotten for him somewhere, a couple of big pods that belonged on a jet pilot. Then he would turn a 45 down to 33 or a 33 to 16 and glue his ear to a speaker while he played along. When he cracked the song he would cock his head, focus on a remote point and hum it to his own accompaniment. It was as though he had some kind of switch in his neck: as soon as you saw his chin tucked into his chest you knew he was unreachable until the fade-out. He had that in common with Billy when he was asleep and Chip when he was swimming: someplace where he was completely himself. I had no such asylum. I had no self.

That struck Teddy as an ironic truth: you were most yourself when you were unconscious, automatic, least insightful. Otherwise occupied. Try to take a good, hard look at your self and it atomized before your very eyes.

In junior high I was befriended by an intellectual kid who had appeared in midyear in my biology class. Given any opportunity he would relate the insults and ripostes of famous people. He was also fond of posing conundrums. Once on the bus home from school he asked me, "Did you ever stop and think that you can't watch your own face?" After a moment's bumpy meditation he added as if knowing my response, "In your case it's just as well."

Then he cackled maniacally. His family moved again before the school year was out.

The Starting Block

It occurred to Ted that the issue of selfhood might also apply to the one sex to which he did not belong. As though in the anti-matter universe he had read about, a couple of girls could be at that moment sitting around a suburban bedroom defining themselves in relation to each other. It was conceivable that Ted's counterpart in that prismatic dimension was Cindy Flood. The girls' behavior would be either complementary to or utterly unconnected with the proceedings in Hooty's room. I. e., Ted might or not be the key to Cindy's identity. In either case, only the superficialities of the scene would differ. The girls would be discussing clothes. The heating register would be on the left.

Having deciphered, and then demonstrated the elusive chord, Hooty was once again incommunicado under his headphones. Actually, only a few chosen records—those containing songs that his band wanted to add to their repertoire—got this close study. Hooty had developed what was without question one of the strangest listening habits in the annals of musical connoisseurship. When he bought a new record, he would carefully slit the cellophane along the open edge of the album with a razor, remove the record and listen to it once. Then he would replace the record in its cover, slide it into his collection, never to be touched again. He claimed this was the only way to simulate the concert experience. This was, of course except for that music her preferred to decipher.

His room was full of non-musical as well as musical gadgets.

Mr. Hurwitz's policy, as paraphrased to me by his son, was not to force interests on his children, but rather to make a variety of activities readily available to them. I witnessed him once walk into Hooty's room and announce almost shyly that he had picked up a ham radio kit that Hooty might want to look at. He had left it on the workbench in the garage.

Since Hooty seemed stuck on a certain passage, time and again lifting the arm of his record player and setting it back to the same starting point, I waved a hand in front of his face.

"Hooty, I'm about to do something dramatic," I said.

"Shoot," he answered, yanking the headphone jack out of his amplifier, so that music blared suddenly from the speakers.

"The least you could do is turn the song off while I make my announcement."

He leaned from the waist to hit the reject on his record player, then righted himself politely.

Although Cindy had no skill that Ted was aware of, he did not doubt that she had a self. In his less disciplined moments, he wondered what it would be like to be a girl, especially a Cindy Flood—to wake up every morning on the inside of that beauty. He had had dreams on the subject.

"I'm going to take Cindy Flood out."

"And?" Hooty said.

"Isn't that dramatic enough for you?"

"Where are you going to take her?"

"I haven't decided."

"That's cool." Hooty said, his fingers were twitching on the keyboard. "Play it by ear. That's what I do."

One bright morning Teddy woke up pressing leafy fingertips against the plate glass window of a greenhouse as he peered outside. It was an odd sensation, because he was the greenhouse. More alarming, he was a girl.

"I haven't asked her yet," I said.

Without a word, Hooty reached into a pile of papers and extracted a telephone. Inside his room he was completely self-sufficient. It wouldn't have surprised me to find a cache of canned food in his closet.

In a flash it dawned on me what he was doing. I threw myself across the floor, clutching for the phone, which I drew underneath my body like a live grenade.

"For the love of the mother of Moses, no!" I cried. I ended up sprawled at Hooty's feet with a nose full of newsprint.

This display was not as dramatic as it might sound. Two or three like it took place between us in the course of most nights. The more trivial the occasion, the more blasphemous the oath it provoked, the harder we laughed. Ordinarily. That night Hooty just gazed at me, Buddha-like, as I prostrated myself before him.

"You were going to call her!" I admonished him, genuinely

stunned.

"I was going to call information," he said. "I don't have her number committed to memory."

"I'm not ready to call her yet," I said. "I need your advice. We need to talk this through , All right?"

Hooty remained impassive and said, "The phone's off the hook."

That explained the beep emanating from my midriff. I sat up and re-cleared a space for myself on the floor.

"First of all," I said, "you don't call a girl from someone else's house."

"Why not?"

"That might seem disrespectful."

"What's she going to do, trace the call?"

"Second, this is not the right time to call."

"It's early," Hooty said. "It's eight-thirty."

"Yes, but it's the wrong night," I explained. "Thursday night is too late to ask her out for this weekend, and Thursday night is obviously too early to ask a girl out for the end of the following week."

"Well, you don't have to ask her out for a weekend. School's out. There is no such thing as a school night."

"On a first date, though."

"I stand corrected," Hooty said, reaching for his headphones.

"Wait a minute," I said. "Where should I take her?"

"Just go over to her house."

"The term is take *out*."

"Then bring her to your house."

Teddy was inclined to forgive Hooty his occasional flippancy.

"I'll take her someplace traditional," I said. "A movie. I'll take her to a movie the weekend after next. I'll call her next Tuesday. I'll consult you again, say, next Monday?"

"Anything I can do to help," Hooty said, switching on the music. Then he fitted himself with the headphones and inserted the jack in the record player.

The sudden quiet reminded me where I was.

"On second thought, maybe I could bring her over here," I said.

Hooty may or may not have heard me.

CHAPTER FOURTEEN

Practice

Ted recognized the irony in the fact that he saw Cindy Flood naked before he so much as touched her.

Theoretically it should be easier to meet a girl over summer vacation than during the school year. But suburban high schools are designed to prevent any occurrence that is either pleasurable or natural or, worse still, both. File around linoleum halls long enough with an armload of books and you begin to behave like a human locker. The most heartfelt thing I ever said to Cindy in the course of a school day was that I had to go to the baker's—bread, not pastry—and I expressed that sentiment in French. That was the one class we had together. No wonder if she thought of me ever since as an intellectual type. Maybe if I had forgotten to use the subjunctive mood.

At the pool you would think all you had to do was pick your way through the bodies strewn over the grass to the jeune fille of your choice and wish her a simple "Ca va." But it didn't work that way at Community Swim Club. Cindy seemed never to arrive unaccompanied, but always with a flock of her newly found friends. Immediately on her arrival in suburban Pittsburgh from the south she had not only found a social niche, but influenced both fashion and speech patterns. These girls would immediately set up an open-air homeroom on the terrace. It wouldn't have surprised me on closer inspection to find they had spread their beach towels in alphabetical order: Baker, Ellis, Flood . . . or maybe a diplomatic compound would make a better analogy than a homeroom. You wouldn't think of approaching one of those girls without a delegation of four or five guys. The less attractive members of the group would greet you and act as interpreters.

Too much sex and too palpably obvious, Ted felt, was the ironic explanation for the social constraints of the pool. Swimming practice, with its striving, half-naked athletes, hips straining against nylon seams, was the perfect, albeit painful, example of this wholesale denial of attraction.

Yes, I am a swimmer, too; the last in a long line of Livingstone freestylers.

But despite Ted's published theory that people in bathing suits were nude, he was not counting swimming practice as his sighting of a

Cindy Flood au naturel.

We were sitting on the deck after warm up on a lucid day in early July. It was going to be an easy workout, the day before the meet with the odious Chapel Gate. I was watching the water shadow I had left when I lay down soak into the concrete and allowing myself an occasional glance at the girls, usually disguised as a sudden, sidelong insight, but in fact an exercise in X-ray vision. If I caught a girl's eye, she might for an instant look as sobered as I was by my thought until she came to herself and looked away.

Maybe the reasoning was that swimmers would naturally assume they were awash, afloat in water rather than sex itself.

For the fiftieth time that day, Susie Baker ran the tips of her index fingers under the seat of her suit, pulling it away from and then smoothing it down over her buttocks, the lower lobes of which had acquired the texture of Moroccan leather from prolonged contact with cement.

Ted and his teammates wore red and white striped tank suits. Not surprisingly, the white stripes were markedly more diaphanous than the red. The vagaries of the textile mill and individual anatomy dictated that every so often the stripes on a girl's suit were aligned in such a way that a white stripe passed over the peak of one or both of her breasts, in which case the specific anatomy showed through in what might seem at first glance a slight factory defect. If a suit were a little too big on a girl she would tie her straps together in back with a shoelace. No one would deny, though no one would point out, that this measure was to prevent her breasts from falling out into plain view.

The concrete on which I hunched was bone-white again by the time my fellow swimmers and I were addressed by our coach, the versatile Ed Gow.

It occurred to Ted that perhaps intensity would be the key to the team's performance the following day.

"All right," Ed said, beginning to pace the deck. "What is the key word for the meet? The key word is intensity."

Still, Ted reflected, perhaps that intensity should be controlled.

"*Controlled* intensity," Ed went on. "That's the real key."

Ed was of the old school: he wore a jock at all times, even under the tank suit he wore for practice, the surface area of which was somewhat smaller than that of the supporter. On him the exposed undergarment was not a particularly sexual statement. Whenever, in the course of his daily lifeguard's duties, he had to enter and exit the pool, his trunks sagged with water, revealing the back of the strap and beneath it a zone of tufted lower spine that looked anything but attractive.

Although the magnitude of Ted's own virility was such that it demanded support as well, he opted for two suits. The top one was fashionably baggy and tattered, commonly referred to among swimmers as a drag suit.

"The Chapel Gate meet is going to be close. You know that as well as I know that," Ed went on. "It always is."

The memory of past defeats seemed to burn like chlorine in his eyes.

"What do the meets come down to? They come down to the relays."

The rhetorical question was important to Ed's pep talks. The fact that he answered every one immediately himself probably detracted from the effectiveness of the technique.

"What about Progar?"

This question, far from rhetorical, was posed with a certain ghoulish satisfaction by Gaffney, our squat, swarthy breaststroker. He could always be counted on for misplaced poolside melodrama.

"We'll let Chip take care of Progar," Ed responded tersely. "We've just got to worry about the relays."

You'd have to say that Coach Gow was begging this particular question, since Progar would undoubtedly be on at least one of the relays, medley and free, at either end of the meet. Chip would face him in the hundred free and anchor our relays. If he beat Progar head-to-head he could presumably beat him the other times as well, but he might start out behind and have to catch him. Our meets with Chapel Gate routinely came down to the final relay.

"Today we're going to do some fifties, then some starts," Ed went on. "That's all. But I want to see some race-type intensity in the sprints, people!"

The Starting Block

This was the most enjoyable kind of practice. Ordinarily we swam in circles, an innovation Chip brought back with him from his AAU workouts. The whole team would be in the pool at the same time, with everybody keeping to the right in his lane. It was like driving in rush hour traffic or, alternatively, like living in a horizontal ant farm. But today we would approach the blocks in heats, by age group, beginning with the girls over sixteen. Everyone else would watch and wait their turn.

The proceedings had a certain oblong, sideways, and shimmering character from Ted's vantage point, as he lay on his back and let his head rock to the side. The covey of girls on the starting blocks scattered at the sound of the gun.

Billy's group took the blocks next. He was not as fast a swimmer as Chip, but he was a more earnest swimmer. In fact, he was the most earnest swimmer I had ever seen. In fact, he swam as earnestly as he slept. As Ed barked his "*Take* your mark," Billy snapped into his crouch. Conserving his blanks, Ed started this heat with his disyllabic "Ho"; when someday in late middle age he retired from the lifeguard's trade he would be qualified to lead wagon trains. The swimmers dropped out of sight as though into another dimension. Foam sprouted from the deck.

From my ground-level view all I could see was Billy's hands, which he looped high in the air with his distinctive straight-arm recovery. I followed them along my low concrete horizon like a pair of diving birds. Billy had never gotten the hang of the classic elbows-high style that Chip had. He had a funny hitch in his freestyle. He breathed every stroke even in a sprint, jerking his head up as though for the last gulp of air in the atmosphere. A single kick followed. Rhythm was not in Billy's vocabulary. You wouldn't think he could swim butterfly, but he rocked his way through the water like a sidecar on a railroad track, up and down, kick and pull. He was just big and strong; he gathered bushels of water with each stroke, and he was tough to beat in either free or fly over a short distance. In the words of a coach I liked to quote to Billy, "A taller fast swimmer will beat a shorter fast swimmer every time, all other things being equal." Of course, they weren't if Billy happened to be racing his slightly shorter, slightly older brother. *And* above four laps Billy faded. In workouts he and I ordinarily swam in the fastest lane, in the middle of the pool. He would start out as lead swimmer and gradually drop back in the pack as practice continued. Endurance was not his long suit.

Billy's hands touched the wall. The moving geysers behind him caught up and died down. He had won the heat.

"Nice job, but don't leave your effort in the workout, guys. The meet's tomorrow night."

By rotating his head 180 degrees on the axis of his neck Teddy could identify the source of this observation, which was neither rhetorical nor nasal enough to originate from Ed Gow. It was his elder brother, Charles, i.e., Chip.

The Starting Block

Now that he was swimming AAU, Chip didn't work out at Community. For the past few years he had been training with an independent club in an Olympic-sized pool in a neighboring suburb. He still swam for our team in summer league meets; and he might show up toward the end of practice, before work, to consult with Ed and kick a little occasional ass in the pool. He might just kid around. But he did inspire the team. When he joined a workout the pool suddenly pounded like a blender turned up from "puree" to "churn." He brought his own kickboard. He wore goggles.

"That's what I was saying," Ed chimed in. "Control that intensity."

I controlled mine very successfully on my heat. It helped that I missed my turn. I touched the wall in the wake produced by everyone else's kick, then looked up to find Chip standing thoughtfully over me on the racing block.

"Is there a fifty-meter body surf tomorrow night?" he asked after a pause.

The timing of Teddy's brother was peerless.

"All right," Ed droned from the deck. "Get yourselves in relay teams and find a lane. Medley," he added over the din that erupted.

I worked my way over to an end lane with Hooty and the other two members of our alternate medley relay. Scrubs, we would swim a couple of lanes over from the official relay in the meet.

"Since Chip is going to anchor both relays, he's going to talk about your starts," Ed continued.

"I don't want to sound negative," Chip said from the block, where he had stayed, "but the first thing to remember is that there are numerous ways to louse up a relay. Especially a medley relay. The stroke people have to keep their form right into the wall. A backstroker can turn over on his stomach when he reaches for the wall, in which case he isn't doing the backstroke anymore and he gets disqualified. A breaststroker can get excited at the end of his leg and duck his head underwater and get disqualified."

Gaffney found some grim humor in this allusion to his specialty and smirked, "It's harder for a butterflyer to get disqualified, but my brother may be able to find a way."

The team recognized this remark as comic relief and tittered. Billy's frown was obligatory. Gaffney smirked again.

"But the most obvious way to screw up is to false start," Chip explained.

In the middle of Chip's lecture, like a delinquent student, I looked around at my teammates. All the guys, even Gaffney, were following Chip's remarks intently, even though they had heard it all before. For once, I looked at the girls without trying to see through their suits. They stood around hugging themselves, watching Chip with open, innocent faces. What difference did it make to them if they swam fast? It didn't make them any more attractive. Even if a girl did swim fast, some guy would swim faster. What mortal enemies did they have at Chapel Gate? The girls there were identical. But tomorrow night they would be jumping up and down and screaming as though their futures depended on the outcome of the freestyle relay. In truth, I felt a little sorry for all of them, girls and guys alike. They were listening to a maniac and didn't know it. All they knew was that Chip was handsome, witty and smart. They never saw him measure peat moss into a glass of milk or set a sit-up board at the angle of basement steps or lob a lamp out his window when he failed before his fiftieth pushup. (He would retrieve it from the honeysuckle the next day.) All they wanted was to care as much as he did. But they never would. He wouldn't let them.

"A flying start in a relay is a tremendous advantage," Chip continued. "It can take a full second off your split. That's why you cannot set an individual world record in a relay."

"A backstroker can," J. T. Orum grinned from the terrace.

Like Chip, he swam AAU and came late to our practice, just before he started guarding.

"Because he leads off," Chip said. "Is that a prediction?"

By way of answer, J. T. stretched his right arm overhead and whirled it around like a propeller in reverse.

"Last year Chapel Gate beat us on the freestyle relay," Chip went on. "Remember? They won the relay by eight tenths of a second. Remember? You *should*. Everybody on both relays is back this year. Our starts were not flying. They were poor. We need to get those seconds back.

"The rules say you're legal as long as your toenails are scraping the block when the swimmer ahead of you touches the wall," Chip continued. "That would be ideal, but you probably shouldn't cut it that quite close. It's a matter of timing. You don't decide when to leave the block, because you can't hold up for a second when you're hanging out over the pool in mid-air. You decide when to start your dive. Then you just go." He bent over, dangled his arms over the deck as though it were the water and looked up at us and added, "Most of you probably start a race like this, with a big arm swing."

When Chip jerked his neck and shoulders, his brother felt a sympathetic twinge in the small of his back.

"I wouldn't do that in a relay," Chip went on. "It's not because it takes longer; it does, but you could always start your dive earlier. It's because it's harder to time. Simplify the motion. Put your hands back here," he said as he laid each of his hands on a hip, palm up, like small wings. "Clasp them behind your back if you want. Then all you have to do is lean at the right time and throw your arms straight out."

As he was demonstrating this motion he tottered, lost his balance and stepped off the block onto the deck. He climbed back up again.

"Don't do that tomorrow night, either," he said. And remember, a false start isn't always caused by the guy on the block. It might be the person in the water's fault if he decides to take another quick stroke instead of stretching for the wall, if he kicks in or if he decides to die at the end of his leg. You have to know your partner. You have to know what to expect from him, but still be flexible. Let's demonstrate the breast stroke-butterfly exchange. That can be tricky. Ed?"

Despite his sunglasses, Ed managed to indicate facially that he couldn't have agreed more that we should demonstrate the breast stroke-butterfly exchange next.

"Gaffney, you'll be swimming breast," Chip said. "Billy, you're doing fly."

Chip stepped down from the block in favor of Billy and moved to the side of the pool opposite most of the team. Gaffney, looking put upon, slouched out of the crowd. When he reached the side of the pool he sprang into the air in a parody of a racing dive, jerking his headway up and landing like a slab, dousing the first couple rows of his teammates. He stopped dead underwater, like a fish sunning itself, then, still submerged, stroked lazily half the length of the pool. He surfaced with his expression unchanged. I wondered idly if he had eyelids.

"Swim it in," Chip said.

Instantly in all seriousness, Gaffney churned for the wall. Billy coiled into position but was rocking back on his heels when Gaffney touched. Gaffney had time to turn knowingly and watch him hit the water before he looked up at Chip.

"I was trying to make it clear that you don't have to shake hands with your partner before you start," Chip said. "Try it again. I wouldn't mind having a lead tomorrow night."

This time Billy false started, not by much, but enough that the team turned as one to wait for Chip's verdict.

"I'd almost rather have you do that than start flat like last time," he said, "except that we would be disqualified. Do it again." He said as he climbed up into a lifeguard's chair to watch.

It was pretty to see when they got their timing down, Billy stretched out parallel for an instant over Gaffney before he punctured the water, then surfaced into the sunlight with three strong strokes before he pulled up in the middle of the pool. You could imagine a relay like that going on forever.

"You get the idea," Chip said to the team at large.

"All right," Ed intoned. "All breaststrokers and butterflyers in the pool. Find a lane."

That gave Hooty and me—a backstroker and a freestyler, respectively—an opportunity for further reflection on the wall by the hedges. I reflected on Cindy. Like birds strutting across a yard, she and the other breaststrokers bobbed their faces in and out of the water as they swam to the wall. All of them, even Gaffney, had that look of wide-eyed anxiety when they breathed. Only on her, it was pretty.

Obviously, Teddy had failed to keep to his telephoning schedule. Nearly a month had passed since he promised his confidant,

Hooty Hurwitz, that he would call Cindy.

On the blocks, one butterflyer after another bent at the waist, as if this were some elaborate ceremony and they were all bowing politely at my big brother, enthroned in his lifeguard's chair.

"Butterflyers, stay in the water," Ed said. "Freestylers, you're on the blocks."

It was my turn to pay my respects.

By the end of the workout Teddy had yet to see Cindy or any other woman naked in the strict sense of the word.

CHAPTER FIFTEEN

A Disconcerting Suggestion

It was all too neat. Though far from paranoid by nature, T. Livingstone noted all the signs of conspiracy as he entered the kitchen one morning a few days and several degrees centigrade farther into the summer. It was not yet nine o'clock, but the windows swelled like sponges with sunlight. Teddy walked carefully, as though the gathering heat could be stirred up like silt. He had already observed the remnants of Chip's pre-workout meal on the countertop, a few orange halves completely drained of juice but otherwise intact. Mrs. Livingstone, who stripped orange sections to the rind with her teeth and left only the seeds and stem of an apple, was always trying to convince Chip that he forewent the best part of a given piece of fruit.

Both Ted's parents were still sitting at the kitchen table, in front of just the beverage for a stifling summer morning—steaming black coffee. As he stepped into the room he was met by their joint gaze.

Teddy was already on edge, due to the unsettling development of the previous night: Cindy had agreed to go out with him. It wasn't the fact per se; it was the eerie sequence of events that led up to it. After several more consultations with Hooty, he had called Cindy on the telephone. Her mother answered. Cindy was home. Ted suggested they go out. She agreed.

This sinister pattern did not end there.

"Isn't that nice," Mom said when I announced the impending date. "Where are you going?"

"Oh, Marge." Dad dropped his head in momentary disgust, but turned it back in my direction for the answer.

"To a movie, I guess."

"Wonderful," Mom said. "What movie?"

"Whatever's playing."

"Well, hadn't you better check the listings?"

Mom looked toward Dad innocently, but he had dropped his face into his hands. The furrowed top of his head frowned at me instead.

"Marge, kids these days don't operate the way we did," he said, surfacing. "They don't go places. What do you think, they go out for dinner and dancing? They just go out,." he said illustrating by shooting his hand laterally into space. "They go!"

"I just think that a little planning ahead would stand you in good stead come tomorrow night," Mom said.

Dad shook his head at me in commiseration.

"You wouldn't want to arrive at the theater tomorrow night only to discover that your young lady had already seen the featured attraction," Mom interposed.

From time to time Ted's mother reminded him that there were people who actually spoke the way they did in commercials. If she felt a sneeze coming on she was very likely to ask him for a facial tissue rather than a Kleenex.

"Four screens," Billy said as he skated across the linoleum floor toward the refrigerator in slow motion, his morning gait, just in time to resolve this point. "I'm assuming you're going to the Cheswick."

Mom looked expectantly at me.

"That's what I'm assuming," I said.

"Assuming?" Mom said. "I wonder what Cindy is assuming."

"The whole idea is to be casual, Marge," Dad said.

"Okay, okay." Mom threw her hands up with a smirk of moronic incomprehension, an expression she had either dredged up from earliest childhood or developed over the past couple of weeks, in either case a sign that the situation in the kitchen that morning was already well out of hand. "And, if I may ask," she resumed, "how will you get there?"

Dad smiled sadly toward Billy and me.

"Is that an unreasonable question?" Mom said.

Ted, who had only recently applied for his learner's permit, conceded that the matter had not come up in his phone conversation with Cindy.

"I didn't expect her to go out with me in the first place," I said. "I thought that was enough to establish in one phone call."

"Why don't you go someplace you could walk? That might be fun."

"Mom, please. I'm trying to eat."

"What is so terrible about that?" Mom asked.

"It's not like the old days, Marge," Dad said. "There are no sidewalks."

"Well, what do they do these days, Mr. Science? Levitate? Wear jet-packs?"

First Ted's father shrugged at him. Then, unprovoked, he turned viciously on him.

"You two could double date," Dad suggested.

Ted and Billy looked at each other without a trace of recognition.

Mom sealed the arrangement by standing up in a sudden huff and saying,. "Oh, let the men solve it all by themselves. I just wish you knew what it feels like to be outnumbered all the time."

Just at that moment Chip walked through the side door into the kitchen. He had probably been dry when he left the pool, but now his tee shirt stuck to his chest in patches, and his forehead was damp with sweat.

"Oh, good," Mom greeted him. "Take your marks, everybody, the relay is complete. Chip is here to swim the anchor leg. Only you false started. Or is it the opposite? Anyway, you're late."

Mom stacked every plate within reach, set them on the counter, and left the room. Dad got up and followed her.

Chip looked around the kitchen at a rare loss and asked. "Am I involved in this?" .

CHAPTER SIXTEEN

A Night at the Pool

Like a humid, human lens, Teddy saw the next two days through a film of sweat. This constant secretion could be attributed in part to the ungodly heat and in part to the blind, elemental fear caused in him by the opposite prospect either of actually being in the same car with Cindy or, conversely, of seeing the date miscarry through illness, a family emergency, or delayed revulsion on Cindy's part. His first impulse was to assume a pseudonym, hire on at the Blaw-Knox mill down on the river, (as it was like an open hearth outside anyway), and work four or five successive shifts until it was time to pick up Cindy. If he remained incognito over the next thirty-six hours he could be sure Cindy couldn't reach him to cancel out, and he could prevent any further developments like the recent spontaneous doubling of the date. Billy was growing quite enthusiastic over the upcoming outing, and that was perhaps Ted's chief worry.

The rest of that Friday, and then Saturday, were just to remind everybody it was July. Heat fell steadily and drifted like sand into our house. You had to lean into the doors to get from one oven-like room into the next. The sky had started out that morning blue and burnished; and by noon it turned a sheetmetal white. Later Friday, after swimming practice, I earned my date money by cutting the Fikes' lawn, as I did every week, wheeling our lawn mower four houses up the street. Just as I cranked up the engine, the sudden exhaust singeing my ankles, Mrs. Fike burst out of her front door and tore down the sidewalk as though I had just detonated her house.

I had to shut the engine back down while she explained to me that it would really be better if I skipped a week, since it was so dry, didn't I know that the lawn didn't need mowed as often (heavy on that "t") in the middle of the summer; but that as long as I was there I could cut the grass, just not as short. Under her supervision, I clicked all four wheels of the mower up one hole. She was the kind of boss I hated, looking over my shoulder at whatever I was doing, making sure I didn't pull any flowers or miss the lamppost with the hand clipper. At least that day she went back inside right away. I could just make out her husband watching television on a sofa behind the murky screens of the porch. Once in a while a soothing whiff of stale cigar smoke reached me. A couple of hours later, as I carried a load of grass clippings toward the compost pile, Mrs. Fike emerged beaming from the porch carrying a little tray that held a navy blue aluminum glass. The glass contained ice water. I could refill it from the spigot by the garage.

The pool was no relief on days like this. By late afternoon the water would be at body temperature, give or take a couple of degrees, despite the oversized faucet that poured at intervals into the deep end under the diving board like an open hydrant onto a city street. I arrived just in time for the four o'clock adult swim. Men and women in trunks and skirted suits lowered themselves into the water as though into the Ganges. The kids tore down to the snack bar or to the courts for a quick game of shuffleboard. Equipment was optional.

The wooly gray heat only got more oppressive as the sun sank. The weak, slanted shade from the trees evaporated before it hit the ground. The occasional twang of the diving board seemed muffled under the gauzy sky.

At five o'clock Chip was due on the shallow end lifeguard stand.

"Someone scrape Gow out of the chair," he said. "Try a spatula."

Chip was closing the pool that night. Just before he took the stand he placed his dinner order with me. As he rose from his deck chair he glanced out the front gate in time to see another Ford Country Squire discharge a pack of children.

"Oh, good," he said. "More kids. They've been coming all day in station wagons, vans. What next? Amphibious armored personnel carriers?"

Some of Chip's best lines hinged on army surplus.

As he left the pool, Ted acknowledged his relief that Cindy wasn't there. Or, if she was, that he had in the crowd a legitimate excuse for not seeing her. At the same time, he recognized the irony that he dreaded meeting the person with whom he had made a date for the following night.

After our family ate I carried Chip's dinner down to him, part of it on a plate covered with aluminum foil and part in a small ice chest. He liked to eat late, sometimes just an hour before closing. I sat next to him at the corner table on the terrace as he spread his meal out. A couple of the dishes I did not recognize from our dinner. There was just one guard up at this point, J. T., in the shallow end; and the throng had finally thinned out slightly. As I leaned back and watched the pool, the underwater lights came on, turning the water turquoise.

Ted loved to witness that nightly event. For an instant he felt about as untouchable as it was possible for him to feel, unless he was actually submerged at the time.

Just before nine a delegation of adults approached Chip; and he agreed to keep the pool open an extra hour, until ten. He probably could have talked them out of it; because he had a way with adults at which I could only marvel in my relative youth. Store clerks would begin by being short with him, and by the end of a transaction sound obsequious. Mostly, he made grown-ups laugh.

"Hey, Coach," a jocular club member with a kid on the swimming team might ask Chip (although he wasn't the coach), "do I make the traveling squad?"

Chip would make a show of thinking this over, then say "Can you change a tire?" to booming laughter.

More than one older member of Community Swim Club with snow-white hair and leathery brow had sought my gaze with manic glee and said, "Is that your brother? He's a good one!"

"It never occurs to them that we might have plans," J. T. muttered as a cheer went up from the water at the announcement over the P. A. system of extended hours.

One of J. T.'s brothers and some of his friends had showed up a few minutes before and were loitering around the front desk looking adult. I had never seen any of them before this. There were a couple of pretty girls in madras shorts and tennis sweaters. One really tan guy wore a *Michigan Swimming* tee shirt. His hair and his teeth were the same shade of white.

"You go ahead," Chip said, smiling toward me. "My assistant and I will close up."

"You're going to join us aren't you?" J. T. asked. " We're going to the Loop. They'll never card you."

"We'll see," Chip said.

"But will *we* see *you*?" J. T. asked. "Oh, man," he sighed after a knowing pause, to which he tossed Chip his whistle as he turned to his friends.

At home that night Chip and I lay around the steamy living room. We had the house to ourselves. I set up the big floor fan so we could both position ourselves directly in front of it, me on the floor and Chip on the couch, but he explained that it worked better if you pointed it out a window.

"I know it seems strange, but that way it sucks air in all the other windows." He explained.

Even with this adjustment the room felt like a bowl of inertia soup to me.

Every so often from outside we heard what sounded like a truncated clap of thunder.

"Idiot skinny-dippers," Chip said, listening. "Why would you sneak into the pool and then go off the diving board? You can hear it a mile away at night. I probably ought to call the cops on them."

"Maybe it's J. T. and those guys."

"J. T?." Chip questioned as he shook his head and laughed softly to himself.

He didn't stir to call the police on the after-hours swimmers. But he did set his book over the arm of the sofa and reach over to turn up the volume of the radio. The Pirates were playing on the Coast.

Chip was what I would call an idiosyncratic baseball fan. He watched or listened to a given game very selectively. He would suffer through a Giant rally, then turn the set off when the Bucs got men on base.

"Chip," I protested in the top of the fifth with two on and two out. "Clemente's coming up."

"That's an ideal time not to listen," Chip said. "Nothing bad can happen in our absence, only something positive. Even if we get no runs, we wear the pitcher down."

"Don't you want to hear if he hits a home run?"

"You wouldn't want him to hit a home run."

"You wouldn't?" I questioned.

"If you clear the bases, it looks like the rally is over."

Chip kept his hand on the knob. I was always very uncomfortable when he turned the radio on in time for me to learn the count but not the batter. I wouldn't know whether to want the next pitch to be a ball or a strike.

"I'm probably the only sports fan in the country pulling for the Orioles in the American league," Chip went on. "No one wants them to repeat. There's such an underdog mentality in the country today."

Teddy lay on the floor floundering in open Sports Illustrateds—*he had yet to locate an article he hadn't already read, but at least the white, glossy pages radiated a little cool—and contemplated his oldest brother. The possibility of double dating with him passed through his mind for an instant before he suppressed it on two grounds. First, it* was inconceivable. Chip was too much his superior in every relevant respect. Second, Chip didn't date. He hung around with friends a lot. Everybody he knew loved him, but he never really went out. Ted didn't know that anyone had ever asked him why not. He was just about to when Chip turned up the volume on the radio. Music came on.

"Commercial already," Chip said. "That's a bad sign."

CHAPTER SEVENTEEN

My Livelihood

Saturday started out as exactly the same kind of day as Friday; I was up in time to see a moist yellow sun low in the sky. The only difference was that I was going to cut our grass instead of the Fikes.' It was really Billy's turn, but I felt a twinge of gratitude in advance for my chauffeur of the evening to come and decided to let him sleep. To Billy, the roar of a lawn mower outside his bedroom window was a lullaby.

Chip Livingstone had long since retired as a cutter of grass, bequeathing that chore to his younger brothers. It was just as well; Teddy could hardly endorse his technique. Chip may have swum fast, but it seemed to take him all day to mow the Livingstone lawn. His mistake, Teddy felt, was to tackle the biggest (back) yard first and to begin by scrupulously cutting under the trees, holding up the lower boughs with his free arm, and going around the garden beds. Then he would cut the grass remaining in the middle of the yard, which Teddy had heard him refer to as the "bread basket," in concentric squares of decreasing circumference. Teddy honestly believed that in his mental map of the day, his brother imagined that he was cutting a swath across the Ukraine. He may well have, under the roar of the lawn mower engine, been chanting Russian folk songs. Finished with the backyard, over the hump, Chip would then dawdle over the rest of the yard, and even trimmed the edges with the hand clippers.

When I mowed our own lawn, I cut a few corners, so to speak. I got the skimpy front and side yards out of the way immediately, then mowed the back, swerving for objects moveable or immoveable. Furthermore, I dispensed with the grass catcher, and I trimmed with the mower itself, setting two wheels on the grass and two on the cement. This method had the added benefit of keeping the edges of the sidewalk and patio beveled; (I was always happy to throw a little masonry in with my gardening.) Dad was far less vigilant a homeowner than Mrs. Fike. He might appear beside me while I stopped to fill the tank with a mixture of gasoline and oil, survey the expanse of grass and remark idly, "You know, a lawn isn't really cut unless it's raked," the way you might say, "Nice day," and with the same results. But he never complained about my work. The price was right.

The Starting Block

Later on at the pool I lay on my back, opening my eyes every so often to check on the sky. Not because I was particularly interested, but because it was directly overhead. By three o'clock huge white clouds appeared, each one with a dark center, like a filled tooth. An hour later, as though the asphalt lake of the parking lot outside was evaporating, the sky was paved over with gray. A gust of cold wind woke me up around five. I sat up to see the guards sprinting along the deck trying to take down the umbrellas before they sailed into the pool, dragging tables and chairs behind them. A second squad came out to collect the garbage cans as the first drops of rain pitted the surface of the water and the clouds rifted with thunder. Clutching their belongings, the crowd funneled through the front gate as though out of an airplane, and in five minutes the guards and I were alone in the pool. The temperature must have dropped twenty degrees. Rain raked the decks.

Ted felt an enormous relief as the heat of the day dispersed. Then he remembered his date that evening and felt a different but equally enormous dread.

CHAPTER EIGHTEEN

A Double Date With My Brother

"So, how long have you and Cindy been going out?" Debbie asked, turning completely around on the front seat of the car to talk to me as though sitting on her knees. "This is exciting."

"It's our first date," I said.

"Billy," Debbie said, although she continued to look at me. "We're making history."

Billy nodded, as much in time to the music as in agreement. Within my circle of friends he and Debbie were regarded as man and wife, they had been going together so long. No one could remember when they hadn't been going together. Debbie was pleasant looking without being really pretty. She had prominent green eyes and a short, convex nose that reminded me a little of a beak, especially when she greeted me in the halls at school, which she dutifully did. As she strutted along peering over an armload of books, you would assume she didn't see you. But then you realized her smile was peripheral, and as you were passing her she would snap out a sideways "Hi" at the last possible second, like a bird snatching a piece of bread out of your hand. As a result, your "Hi" in response inevitably sounded a little lame.

"How did you meet?" Debbie asked.

I had to think for a minute, and then I said, "I guess we never *met*. I just called her up a couple of nights ago."

Debbie's eyes widened, and I could see it was going to be difficult to disappoint her that night.

"This gets better and better," she said.

A related or maybe an opposite habit that Debbie had was to fix me with a sidelong, privately meaningful stare in the midst of a larger social function. If she came over to our house to spend an evening I was liable to turn at the dinner table and find myself impaled on her gaze, which I always tried to return for as long as humanly possible. She indulged this proclivity for the next two miles, until we turned through the brick pillars into Cindy's neighborhood. At that point she turned around and smoothed herself into the passenger's seat. "KQV is playing good music tonight," she said to Billy.

I had prepared a few opening remarks for Cindy's parents, but

Cindy answered the door. The whole house seemed deserted; the living and dining areas were combined into one high-ceiling, cavernous room behind her. It had the air of a meal adjourned for a generation or so. I had a sudden vision of Cindy at the massive table flanked by much older brothers, home from law school, maybe a married sister. The vague sound of a television seemed to have risen into the rafters earlier that evening and stayed there. Cindy greeted me brightly and grabbed her purse.

As soon as Billy turned the engine over Debbie swiveled back around in her seat and asked Cindy all the same questions she had asked me. Our date seemed still more miraculous to her on second hearing. Billy was even less help to me than I had expected. He seemed to think of himself exclusively as chauffeur/disk jockey for the evening. I knew from experience that he prided himself on deciding after a millisecond whether he liked a song or not. He worked the buttons on the radio like typewriter keys, punching through them until he found an acceptable number, then he sat back and drove contentedly. Luckily, Debbie and Cindy had a lot about which they could talk. They had both been born in Miami, among other things.

"I don't believe this," Debbie kept saying.

Eventually, Ted sat back in his seat behind his brother and watched Route 28 unravel alongside the Allegheny River. Dusk was settling over a misty landscape of gray and green. The nearest movie theaters were in the next mill town upstream, and Ted found something comforting in the body shops they passed, the small businesses with their shallow cinder parking lots. Lives were led there, though not at the moment. Down by the river even the asphalt was fertile; parsley-like grass and small shrubs grew right out of the curbs and driveways.

Once we got to the theater we opted for *Bonnie and Clyde*. There wasn't really much of a choice; the other titles included a full-length animated feature and a foreign film that Debbie and Billy had already seen. "When?" I felt like asking, and then, "Why?" Although the auditorium wasn't crowded, I maneuvered the group so that I sat on an aisle, with easy access to the concessions. I couldn't trust Billy to cover that angle. Plodding behind the others down the aisle gave me a familiar heavy-footed sensation, as though in the depths of the dim theater I was wearing a deep sea-diving suit. Soon I was mired in a spongy, springy seat. Nonetheless, I got up twenty minutes or so into the movie to fetch the traditional refreshments, a bucket of popcorn which, for an extra quarter could be saturated with butter, and soft drinks mixed before my eyes at the machine from separate streams of factory fresh chemicals in a clear plastic cup. They must have been out of test tubes. I timed my arrival back at the seats to coincide with the movie's first major bloodbath.

"What's that?" Billy asked as I balanced all the containers on my lap.

"What do you think it is?" I said, looking past the parallel profiles of the girls at my brother.

Ted had noted before that, though openly revolted by a proffered foodstuff, people always made a show of urgency as they passed it on for the next person to enjoy.

The girls relayed the popcorn between Billy and me. I ended up eating the bulk of it.

"Good flick," Billy said, jingling his keys as we walked out onto the sidewalk afterwards.

It was dark by then, and there was a line waiting for the next show. It contained a number of sport coat wearing adults to whom Ted felt slightly superior.

Billy did a funny thing in the parking lot. He went straight to the door on the driver's side and opened it. Then he looked across the top of the car and saw all three of us on the other side.

"Billy," Debbie said. "Where are your manners?"

"Uh-oh," he said. "A fatal faux pas."

Suddenly he doubled over and began to jerk in slow motion, buffeted by imaginary machine-gun bullets, Clyde in his death throes. He fell across the front seat and, with his dying gesture, opened the door for Debbie.

Cindy laughed. So did I.

As we pulled back out onto Route 28 I asked, "Is there someplace open to eat?"

No one seemed to know offhand. After a moment of silence Debbie twisted around toward me and said, "Didn't you get enough popcorn?"

Cindy watched the windshield as intently as she had the movie screen.

The question remained unresolved, because almost immediately the car developed some sort of trouble. Billy eased off the highway into the parking lot of a motel, excused himself, and went around behind the car. From inside we could hear a few dull thuds.

"Just checking," Billy said when he was back behind the steering wheel, but a mile later he stopped again and got out.

The third time he pulled over onto a side street. I got out and joined him back by the trunk. He was frowning down at the left rear tire.

"What's the matter?" I asked.

Billy took his hands off his hips long enough to deliver a couple of solid kicks to the tire.

"Are you having a good time?" he asked.

"This is my first date," I said. "Am I supposed to have a good time?"

"Yes, you're supposed to," Billy said. "That's the object of a date. It's an opportunity for you to get to know someone a little better, to see if you get along. Just for the evening—you don't have to propose when you drop her off. I get the feeling you think there's some kind of formula Cindy expects you to follow. Are you *really* hungry?"

"Are you kidding? The next time I see anything buttered I'll vomit."

"Do you have any reason to think Cindy is hungry?"

"No."

"Then don't eat. You don't *even* have to go to a movie," he said as he held up a palm to ward off an apology. "I don't mean I didn't enjoy the movie. I kind of follow Penn's films. I just mean you don't have to go anyplace special. You can just spend time together."

Teddy paused and weighed this advice. Then he asked if there was anything he could do to help with the car.

"Sure," Billy said, chewing his lip, his eyes back on the ground as he was at his most cryptic when he needed a favor. "Watch the tire while I kick it."

"All right," I said. I guess you learned all this about dates from Chip."

"We haven't discussed the subject. I assumed he was saving all his wisdom for you," Billy said, repositioning himself slightly. "Stand back a little. Closer to the front of the car."

When I moved back I was flush with the rear window. I shrugged to the girls. After I observed the impact of Billy's foot on the tire I said, "It looks all right."

"I know," he said.

Then it dawned on Ted.

"There was never anything wrong with the tire," I said. "You just wanted to get me alone to give me that advice."

Teddy was touched, and he said so.

"Not exactly," Billy said. "Popcorn makes me fart."

Billy had parked under a big, leafy tree. Lit by a street lamp, it cast its cone of shade upward into the night. When we were back inside the car, Billy twisted in the driver's seat and for the first time that evening spoke directly to Cindy.

"Young lady," he began, "I realize I know you only very slightly, through my brother here, but may I ask you a few questions?"

"Yes," Cindy said tentatively.

Ted watched her features assume the expression of incredulity that he had extolled more than once to Hooty, expressions he had been unable to induce all evening.

As soon as Cindy had given him permission to address her, Billy turned back around and spoke to the steering wheel. "Can you stay out a little later?" he asked.

"I suppose so," Cindy replied.

"Till six A. M., would you say?"

At this Debbie grimaced.

"Probably not that late," Cindy said in a measured way, as her look of disbelief grew.

"All right, I can appreciate that," Billy said, gazing out the windshield and tapping the steering wheel with his fingertips as though it were a lectern. "Cindy?"

"Yes?"

"May I ask you a more personal question?" Billy adjusted the rearview mirror so that he could look her in the eye.

"Go ahead." Cindy laid a hand on the inside of my elbow to keep from laughing. Debbie had buried her face in her hands.

"Do you have a dollar?"

"Yes."

"Do you have two dollars?"

"Yes."

"Would you like to look in your purse before you give your final answer?"

"No, thank you." First she shook her head, then she nodded it. "I'm sure I have two dollars."

"Cindy, I want to thank you for your cooperation and your candor," Billy said as he started the car, did a quick U-turn and put us back out on Route 28.

"Billy," I asked after a glance around at the girls, "where are we going?"

We seemed to be heading home.

"We're here," Billy said, pointing off to his right and hitting the turn signal.

Beyond the body shops and the four store shopping centers, set back against the mined-out cliffs, stood Laura Lanes.

"Bowling?" I asked.

The Starting Block

"*All-night* bowling," Billy said. "Ten PM to six AM for a buck." After he parked, he turned off the ignition and spun toward the back seat and said, "Don't worry—Cindy's paying for it."

As they stepped into the Lanes, Ted had to admit that, ridiculous as he considered the activity, the facility inspired awe. He hadn't been inside this place since cub scouts, but the grandeur of it had not been diminished by the passage of time. Past the acres of red carpet that greeted them, sixty lanes stretched out under the scalloped white roof to vanishing points in either direction. The crack of falling pins, and the rumble of bowling balls on hardwood blended into a sustained though muffled roar. It was like an indoor airport.

"Now. Ted?" Billy asked. "Do you have fifty cents?"

"Of course I do."

"Do you have two fifty cents'?"

"Yes."

"Then you two get the shoes for you and Cindy," he said as he handed Debbie a dollar bill for the two of them. "Cindy and I will select a lane."

We ended up on the far left, in the single-digit lanes. To one side of us, a group of several men and women took up two lanes. They all wore pale blue shirts that read "Sixth UP." To the other side was a party of four men. At regular intervals a guy with a gray crew cut yelled, "One time, Burt!" We played teams most of the time. To keep things interesting, Debbie played with me. She and Billy had obviously spent some evenings here; they kept score. Cindy played a deliberate game, slightly out pointing me. We all thought I might be setting some kind of record for strikes followed immediately by gutter balls.

Ted recorded his biggest laugh of the night when, trailing Cindy and Billy by a prohibitive margin late in the second game, he took his approach carefully, then rolled his ball the length of the gutter.

"I figured if I started it down the gutter it might jump out halfway down," he quipped, but by that time everybody was laughing at everything.

As the second stage of their double date unfolded, Ted watched an eerie metamorphosis come over his brother. Billy was transformed from the taciturn, if pleasant, functionary of earlier in the evening to a blue-collar bon vivant. He seemed suddenly in his element. From somewhere he had gotten hold of a snap-brimmed straw hat and a bowling glove. But there was something else. While Ted was certainly delighted that the evening was turning out so well, he was alarmed to witness his brother, like some time-lapse embryo in biology class, turning into a person. Teddy had no control over the process, which reached a peak when Billy came back from the vending machines and set down some drinks and shiny bags of chips on the table. His lips were curiously extended by a cigarette!.

"Billy," I said shocked, as the rest of us sat down. "Swimmers don't smoke."

"Am I swimming?" he asked, holding up a hand to display his bowling glove.

"Seriously," I said. Then, to Debbie, "Does he do this often?"

She laughed, then shrugged.

"Actually," Billy said, "I've always secretly admired athletes who smoke. You know, the guy who runs a good mile in a meet, then lights up. Doesn't that kind of guy impress you, Cindy?"

"Oh, absolutely," Cindy said, straight-faced.

Without another word, Billy pushed the pack of cigarettes across the table toward me.

He did things like that all night long.

At eleven-thirty I went with Cindy over to the pay phone by the entrance so she could call home. We walked underneath the din as though it were a canopy.

"Sometimes I wish I had a brother," she said as we headed back to our lane.

"That's funny," I said. "I pictured you with several older, very protective brothers. Who might be waiting for me when I dropped you off."

She smiled. "Close. A younger sister."

Back at our table, Cindy announced that she could play one last game adding, "But first, now that we're all together, I want to give Teddy a thank-you gift for this nice evening."

The Starting Block

Teddy sat down as instructed and closed his eyes. A minute later he heard laughter and felt a weight settle onto his thighs. In addition to its mass, the object had a couple of other attributes, such as smoothness and coolness, which had become familiar in the course of the evening. It was Cindy's first big laugh, though Ted suspected it had been made possible only by Billy's earlier successes. Doing his part, he gazed speechless with gratitude at the bowling ball in his lap.

We dropped Cindy off first. On her front porch, before I could say a word, she raised her chin to kiss me on the cheek.

Mom greeted Billy and me at the front door of our darkened house in her bathrobe.

"Well," she asked. "Did you have a good time?"

Billy walked past her without a glance in any direction other than that of our bedroom down the hall.

"We went all-night bowling," he said. "Although obviously we didn't bowl all night."

"Obviously?" Mom said, turning her standard mystified look toward me.

"He doesn't mean it the way it sounds, Mom," I said.

"All right," she said. "Did you have a good time anyway?"

"Yes, Mom," Billy and I said in unison.

Teddy was the only one who seemed surprised.

CHAPTER NINETEEN

I Guard My Brother's Life

How romantic, Ted thought as he woke up the next morning. He turned dreamily from his back onto his side, laid a hand to his face and said to himself, "I can still feel the pressure of Cindy's lips on my cheek." However, closer inspection traced this sensation to the zipper on his pillowcase. Eight hours' steady application of skin to steel had produced a T-shaped gouge just to the east of his mouth. He had to remind himself that scars were traditionally manly.

He found his brother Chip sitting alone at the kitchen table looking very adult, sipping a glass of orange juice made unnaturally viscous by several additives, the Sunday paper opened in front of him. A glance at the clock over the sink confirmed that it wasn't any later than Teddy thought it was.

"Why aren't you at practice?" I asked.

"No practice today," Chip said. "Their pool is closed. Some kind of maintenance. Great time for it."

Chip was obviously annoyed at this interruption of his training, but he was distracted for the moment by the season-to-date batting statistics in the fine print of the sports page. Missing a workout made him as testy as a late-inning Pirate loss. I sat down gingerly at the table with my own glass of orange juice. I wasn't often called on to console my eldest brother.

"Actually, it is a good time," I tried. "You'll be rested for tomorrow night."

On Monday night the first of our annual grudge matches with Chapel Gate was to take place, at their pool. What occurred before these meets constituted the most enjoyable part of the season. We would show up at the pool knowing that all we were going to do was practice starts and turns and sit cross-legged on the deck for the duration of Ed's pep talk.

The age-group team Chip worked out with one suburb away was on an entirely different schedule. That was why it was such a concession for Chip to compete in Community's meets; he appeared "by courtesy," like a recording artist. On the other hand, the opportunity, or rather sacred duty to beat Progar and Chapel Gate, was probably enough to insure his presence on the starting block. All the big AAU meets fell toward the end of the summer, after Community's season was over, starting locally and leading up to the nationals. Theoretically, you could fly out to California or down to Florida and get your picture in *Swimming World*, although no one we knew or knew about ever made the qualifying times. When these swimmers eased up in mid-August they called it "tapering" and went about it in earnest. All season long they swam ceaselessly in circles, turning the pool over like a turbine, only to be transformed for a week into torpid couch sloths, lying around on their backs in darkened rooms, the shades drawn, occasionally reaching out feebly to change the channel on the television set or grope on the coffee table for some form of carbohydrate that didn't have to be digested too strenuously.

The night before their big meet they would rouse themselves to perform one of the more nauseating rituals Ted personally had ever heard of. Last year, for the couple of days beforehand, Chip and his friends kept alluding to an upcoming "G & S party." Ted assumed they were confidently planning a victory celebration. "Goggles and Suits?" "Gin and Soda?" "Geishas and Strippers?" It turned out that the party occurred before the meet and that the initials stood for "Gillette and Schick." On the premise that they were cutting down water resistance, they shaved all the hair off their bodies below their necks and outside their tank suits. And they did it together. Ted had walked in on a group of them in the act in their bathroom. J. T. sat in his tank suit in the tub, one lathered leg daintily extended while he shaved it. His pendulous calf was so sharply defined you might think he had just carved it out of flesh with the razor. Chip and Al Strange stood at the sink working on their chests with electric clippers. Ted got out of there just as Chip knelt to take a swipe across J. T.'s back. Later, back in levis, the depilated swimmers walked bow-legged around the living room. *"Feel the draft?"* J. T. laughed. *"I could get into this."*

"No workout for the *team*," Chip said, turning the page. "What are you doing right now?"

"It's nine-thirty Sunday morning." I said. "What could I be doing?"

Not surprisingly, Chip was prepared to answer that question. Five minutes later, a piece of toast in one hand, I was following him down the path to the pool. Despite the previous evening's storm, the weather hadn't cleared up. Although the air was tranquil at ground level, the sky churned violet and gray. It must have rained again during the night. Wet patches lay on the streets we cut across like sweat stains on a shirt. The slightest brush against an overhanging branch left me soaked.

"Are you opening up today?" I asked.

I still wasn't sure what we were doing. Every so often the lifeguards' rotation called for Chip to report for work at eleven, an hour before the pool opened, to set up. That was an airtight excuse for missing church when we were going to church, but we were an hour early even for that.

"I doubt very seriously anybody will want to swim on a day like this," Chip said. "They'll close up early. They may not bother to open."

Chip's use of the third person did not suggest the guard on duty, but he certainly seemed proprietary when he pulled out a bunch of keys and opened the club's side door. The sudden throbbing of the pumps stepped out like a pair of bouncers we had to shoulder our way past into the crowded gloom of the guards' room. The murmurs and gratings of the filter room below were the only invited guests at this party. A swimming club after hours, or before, is an eerie place. A fluorescent desk lamp didn't do much to dispel the darkness, much less the dankness, of our immediate surroundings. Outside, on the deck we found a disassembled summer. Extra chairs were stacked against a wall; the closed-up umbrellas lay beside them like furled sails. The water was glassy smooth; and the bottom of the pool, with its painted lanes, seemed to have come loose like the label on a bottle to float just beneath the surface.

Chip opened the door to the equipment room between the rest rooms with another key. He looped a lane line over my shoulder, and handed me the set of plastic numbers.

"How high can you count?" he asked, reaching down for a lane line for himself. We had one more stop to make, the manager's office, where Chip rummaged around in the desk for a stopwatch and a tablet.

"Time trial?" I asked as I trailed the metal clip at the end of the lane line along the deck, the first in a series of stupid questions.

Chip uncharacteristically passed over an opening for sarcasm, by simply nodding.

"Do you really need the lane lines?" I asked, though only after they were installed. "There's no one else in the pool."

"Absolutely," Chip said. "As close to meet conditions as possible."

I carried the lap counter around to the far end of the pool, just like in a meet, where I would shout out the odd-numbered lengths as Chip turned. Nestling the points of my buttocks in the concrete of the deck, I sat and watched my brother warm up, always a pleasure. He invariably began with a few ritual lengths on his back, stretching his arms out languidly, all but dislocating his shoulder with each stroke. Then he switched to freestyle, picking up his pace gradually, coming out of each fluid turn a little faster than he went into it. He wasn't one of these guys with the showy, straight-legged flips who seemed to think the object was to produce as loud and as large a splash as possible when you turned. That was a definite plus from a counter's point of view.

Ordinarily, Chip would do some kicking and pulling; but today he seemed anxious to begin his time trial. After a few hundred meters he coasted to a stop in front of me and squatted up to his shoulders in the water, bobbing, like a car idling.

"Now," he said. "I'm going at least a thousand, but if I feel good I'm going to keep going. I'll decide five hundred at a time. Do you know how to take splits?"

He had given me the crown jewel of stopwatches, a heavy, ovoid affair of glass and metal, studded with buttons.

"The one on the left is for the split," Chip said. "Hit that after each twenty lengths, record the time, then clear it. Get my split after each *five* hundred. Okay?"

I chose that moment to ask stupid question number two. Or was it three?

"Why are you doing a time trial the day before the Chapel Gate meet? Shouldn't you be resting?"

A sudden image of Progar in repose, sullen and heavy-lidded, came to Ted.

"I have to swim through these league meets," Chip said. "My season hasn't started yet."

Next stupid question. "

"We're not really supposed to be doing this, are we, Chip?" I asked realizing I had felt vaguely uneasy since we left the house. "What if Mr. Caldwell shows up at the pool?"

"I'll get us out of it," Chip said. "Anyway, you've completed senior lifesaving, right?"

Ted's answer was something less than affirmative.

"Oh, well," Chip said, with one last, slightly reproachful

rinsing-out and replacing of his goggles. "Just make sure no one stops me, under any circumstances. That's as important a part of your job as counting."

He glanced toward the sky. What he could see through his blue-tinted lenses I didn't know.

"I'd better get going before it rains," he said. "You might get wet."

He pushed off for the other end of the pool while I set the counter up to the left of the lane, where I would plunge it into the water as I simultaneously shouted the lap number into the vortex of Chip's flip turn. With an artesian gush, as though springing from the bedrock beneath the bottom of the pool, Chip pulled himself out of the water and onto the block in one smooth motion.

"Start me!" he yelled.

"All right!" I yelled back, hefting the stopwatch. "On three!"

"No, *start* me!"

"All right," I barked. "Brothers and timers ready."

It was a mild yet risky witticism on Ted's part, given the seriousness of the occasion. The correct phrase was "Judges and timers ready." *As Chip stepped to the front of the block, the merest ripple of irritation washed up at Ted's feet twenty-five meters away.*

"*Take* your mark," I went on.

Chip bent at the waist, hands dangling, taking position.

"Go!"

Halfway down the first length Chip had already hit his stride, his elbows rising and falling like pistons, a flutter of feet behind.

"One," Ted yelled dutifully, one arm in the water up to his shoulder, although he was reasonably sure Chip hadn't lost count yet. He wasn't sure he ever did.

I sat back on the deck to relax for thirty seconds or so and set the stopwatch in my lap. Briefly it brought back the sensation of a bowling ball.

In the next instant Teddy realized what had been making him edgy ever since Chip announced the project of a long time trial. It wasn't the impropriety, not to mention hypocrisy, since Chip had disapproved of the late night skinny-dippers sneaking into the pool when it was closed or the threat of apprehension by the manager, Teddy's prospective chemistry teacher and employer, Mr. Caldwell. It was something else. His brother wasn't two hundred meters into his swim before Ted heard the first rumblings of thunder.

The clouds had seemed innocuous enough when we walked down to the pool that morning, swirling but flimsy as smoke. Now, as I winced toward the horizon, black stained the overcast sky like ink. There was another roll of thunder, the sound all lifeguards loved. On a normal day the slightest rustle was enough to clear the pool. Chip and the other guards joked about it constantly. They claimed to pick up the crackle of static electricity if a girl in a nylon suit squirmed in her chair. They readied their whistles if they sensed low pressure over

Indiana.

But it was no laughing matter for Ted as he sat and watched his brother knife his way through empty gray water.

I had a clear choice in front of me. If I let Chip swim, he could be electrocuted before my eyes. If I stopped him, even just to warn him, I would ruin his time trial and face his wrath. Brutus or Judas. Take my pick.

So as Ted watched the lightning, at first no more than sparks in a pile of distant black clouds, draw nearer, an unearthly calm settled over him. There was nothing he could do, except his job, which was to see to it that no one and nothing prevented Chip from swimming into his destiny. Prayer was out of the question; it would just alert the Prayee to the fact that they were not in church on Sunday morning. Knowing that he was seeing it for the last time, Teddy could watch his brother's stroke, which by now seemed as inevitable as a square or a circle or some other ideal geometric form, with all the more tenderness. It was fitting and proper that that flawless freestyle be framed by an angry, envious universe. He could only hope for the same setting as he carried his brother's body, singed and inert, back up the hill to their house in his arms.

From the side, you can't understand how a good swimmer breathes. His mouth seems at most half out of the water. Actually, his motion creates a slipstream alongside his body and hence a pocket of air he can breathe.

Ten minutes later, as lightning marbled the sky overhead, Ted felt a twinge of hope. Chip was coming up on a thousand. Silently, Ted implored his brother to conclude his swim; then he watched the soles of Chip's feet flip out of the water like two salmon at the far turn.

"Forty-one."

I wondered again what went on behind Chip's flat, blank lenses. What did he see from inside that private prism of his? What did a person think about while he was swimming as fast and as far as he could? I knew I wasn't in Chip's watery field of vision; he was looking straight ahead, oblivious to any element but water, racing time to see which of them could reach the future first.

The veins that stood out against the knobby clouds reminded Ted of those on the side of the noses of certain elderly acquaintances of his.

Presumably lightning was one of the circumstances under none of which, I was supposed, was to stop Chip.

Ted examined the stopwatch, with which he had just recorded the thousand split, for a button that would work in reverse, stopping the world while time continued. Through and beyond the cyclone fence around the club lay an eternal vision of normality. Houses in neat rows, second stories of bright white siding, trusty station wagons parked half in and half out of garages, like dogs on thresholds. Families were finishing late breakfasts; the men folk were easing the sports section out of the Sunday paper like a wedge of pie. In the schoolyard next door, the jungle gyms and seesaws of Ted's youth swarmed with emptiness. If only he could seize the moment to fix his brother in one everlasting breath under the crescent of his arm raised in mid-stroke, his own cheek luminous like the dial of a watch with last night's kiss, before a bolt of lightning turned the pool into a chlorinated deep fry.

There was another way, it occurred to Teddy when he could no longer have slipped a beach towel edgewise between a flash of lightning and the ensuing clap of thunder. He felt sure the office must contain some appliance, if not a blender then a good-sized clock radio, and he knew he had seen extension cords in the equipment room. The keys lay on top of Chip's sweatshirt. As honor dictated, and under any atmospheric conditions, he could plug in the appliance, turn it on "high" or "loud," depending, carry it down to the pool and jump in to float lifeless alongside the bloated corpse of his brother.

With that resolve, Ted was far from dismayed to see his brother flip at the 1500 for still another five hundred meters. He was resigned. He was amused. He waited for the fatal bolt of lightning to fall, laughing a bitter laugh into the wind in his face as the rain fell on the pool in clods like dirt on a coffin.

A few minutes later the storm was over. Rain hissed in the sudden silence. Then it stopped. Across the pool from me, at the end of his eightieth length, Chip thrust his hand into the wall with a splash and pulled up. I stopped the watch. Without a pause, he threw himself onto his back and stroked leisurely to my end.

"What did I do?" he said, goggles up.

When Teddy read off his time and his splits, Chip laid his head back in the water as though it were a pillow and beamed.

"Good thing I swam fast," he said. "It really is going to storm."

CHAPTER TWENTY

The Meet

You could calculate the score of a summer-league meet all different kinds of ways. You could count boys versus girls, under versus over twelve; even age group by age group. But these methods always struck Ted as rationalizations. There was still a final score. One club won, the other lost. You belonged to one club or to the other.

The whole team felt the gravity of the occasion when we swam Chapel Gate, but each individual swimmer showed it in a different way. A few hours earlier, in sloping sunlight, we had piled out of station wagons and filed down the steep asphalt walk into Chapel Gate, draped in beach towels and carrying bags like a bunch of bewildered tourists on a package vacation. The youngest kids were just scared stiff, wide-eyed and walking into each other; the girls arrived in jabbering clutches. On the other hand, every self-respecting male from the age of twelve up managed a little bravado. That required above all not seeming quite sure whether some of the objects we passed on the grounds might not be girls.

Billy, Hooty and I and a couple of other guys were walking in a loose phalanx through the club later when, at a burst of laughter from the pool deck, we sighted Progar. They must have held some kind of ceremony out here whenever Progar finished his warm up. He was shrugging on his sweats over by a ladder in the deep end, surrounded by a bunch of amused teammates. He was always a little smaller than you remembered, but more solid. One guy stepped back from the group and laughed so hard he seemed to be nodding, but not at us. We had lost the first event, the nonchalance relay. They were definitely the more oblivious of their opponents' existence.

Chapel Gate had been built a couple of years after Community, at the other end of the township. No one would confuse either of them with either of the two country clubs in between. Chapel Gate had kept the classic L-shaped pool, but added what seemed to Ted some tasteless flourishes. What was the point of having two low diving boards, one on either side of the high dive? You didn't need big chrome rails alongside them, either, or a pair of asphalt tennis courts on a lower level. Their locker rooms were concrete and plywood, just like Community's; but the walls were stained red and the bottom of the pool was painted so that the water was unrealistically blue. Who wanted to belong to a post card? The walls of their pavilion were lined with vending machines like ushers, including one for ice cream. One girl at the snack bar did nothing but operate the grill.

As we worked our way through the club we bumped into an occasional acquaintance from school. Your first instinct was to shake hands.

Community had been assigned a patch of lawn on the far side of the deep end, up against one fence, and three lanes for warm up. That was always thirty minutes of chaos. With everybody in the pool at the same time you could usually get in about three strokes before you had to jerk upright to avoid a collision. Gaffney approached warm up with his usual theatrical air of resignation. All he ever did was one breast stroke start after another, dragging himself up onto the block and sizing up his audience peripherally before he sprang suddenly out over the water in his flying squirrel dive, limbs splayed, to land flat-out with a smack. Ted was always surprised he didn't stick to the surface of the water. In the middle of the pool Billy would walk a few steps, burst into his butterfly, and pull up again. Chip was stroking smoothly through the traffic of the middle lane.

In the other half of the pool, Chapel Gate's coach was starting waves of twenty-fives. There was something to be said for showmanship. Progar was on the terrace in his sweats talking to a group of adults.

"What was he", Ted wondered, "the host?"

On every patio parents were shifting their chairs for a good view; mothers wore stopwatches around their necks like pendants. Mr. and Mrs. Livingstone, who had driven out a bunch of younger kids, were in the crowd someplace. Chip had driven the family's other car, while Billy and Ted came out with Hooty.

One of Ed's pep talks was as good a time as any to take stock of your life. After warm up I huddled with the rest of the team on the grass in tuck position, wrapped in a beach towel and holding my knees to my chest. I was afraid that if I let go, not just my teeth but my bones would start to chatter. I looked around at my teammates, uniformly somber for once, and wondered how we had maneuvered ourselves into this position, turning a pleasant summer evening into an excursion into hell. In a matter of minutes I would be standing on a starting block, suspended over a void of screaming voices. The lane lines would stretch away from me like so many tightropes. Hooty sat next to me with a bloody mouth, stained red with cherry Jello eaten right out of the box, a supposed source of quick energy, for me an even quicker source of nausea. I waved away the powder he offered to me mechanically. Off to my right, Chip sat in meditation, head bowed under a towel. It was some consolation to me that I wasn't the one facing Progar. Billy was beside Chip in jeans and a tee shirt. He had developed the pre-race mannerism of changing back into street clothes after warm up, then running to the locker room to put on a dry suit before his first event. When that happened to be the medley relay, which opened the meet, he had to hustle.

It gave me a jolt to see Cindy's face among the girls. I had called her once since our date and seen her a few times around the pool; but we seemed to have an understanding that we wouldn't socialize at practice. She was listening to Ed raptly. Actually, she looked scared. I didn't know why. As far as I knew she was swimming only one event, the fifty, behind Denise Matthews, who was to the girls what Chip was to the boys, a year-round AAU swimmer who was not allowed to be beaten. But there was no female version of Progar.

Although Ed's pep talks were among the most trite ever delivered, Teddy couldn't help but sympathize with him on these occasions. He was invariably interrupted before he could establish a true monotone by one of Gaffney's melodramatic questions or comments. Gaffney showed unusual restraint that night, waiting until Ed was several sentences into his speech before he spoke up.

"How are they using Progar?" he smirked in the general direction of everyone.

"We'll know after the first relay," Ed said grimly.

These summer league meets were much simpler than an AAU or a high school meet. There was really just one individual event, a freestyle race in every age group, girls and boys: one length (twenty-five yards or meters, depending on the club) for the youngest kids; two lengths for older kids; four for the oldest boys. The meets began and ended with four relay races: medley relays at the outset for boys and girls under and over twelve, freestyle relays for a finale. Still, there was a lot of strategy involved. First of all, though theoretically everyone should be eligible for three events—your age group race and two relays—you were only allowed to enter two. That was so as many kids as possible got a chance to swim, and also so a team couldn't win a meet with just a couple of standout swimmers. After public consultation with Chip, J. T. and a couple of the other team elders, Ed had announced at practice the day before that Billy would swim in both relays—butterfly on the medley for boys over twelve, and then third man in the freestyle relay, which Chip would anchor. Chip would also swim the hundred free, presumably against Progar.

"Did Progar warm up butterfly?" Gaffney asked, looking at Billy. Gaffney would be swimming the breaststroke leg right in front of him on the medley relay.

The most maddening thing about Gaffney's questions was that they usually had a point.

"He was done warming up by the time we got here," I offered.

Chip shot a hooded glance at me.

"Any way you cut it," Ed said, "it would be very advantageous to win the medleys."

The scoring of a swimming meet opened up still more strategy. In the individual events, first place got five points, second place three, and third place one. Even if your opponents took first place, your team would only lose a point if your swimmers took second and third. The relays were all or nothing affairs: seven points to the winner and zero to the loser. As a result, you could seem way behind before the last relay and still come back to win the meet; conversely, final scores were often closer than they looked. It was always a temptation to "stack" your relays with all your best swimmers—especially the first one, so you got a big lead. It was risky to swim Billy in place of Chip, who was our best butterflyer as well as our best freestyler, in the medley relay, but we *were* saving Chip for the last relay, on the assumption that Chapel Gate was saving Progar as well.

Apparently that was the conclusion of the pep talk, but as everyone stirred and stretched J. T. sprang to his feet.

"I'd just like to add one thing to Coach Ed Gow's observations," he said as he jerked his thumb toward the other side of the pool. "I don't like these guys."

That brought down the house. We rose and surged in a single wave around Ed and J. T. and began the club cheer. Billy sprinted for the locker room.

The twelve-and-under relays were not always that bad. Naturally, they had all twelve-year-olds on them. Chapel Gate boasted a child prodigy butterflyer, a poker-faced little girl in a wooly blue sweat suit covered with patches from her past AAU meets. She won the first medley relay for them single-handedly with a precociously smooth stroke. But we took the next two relays and had a good chance to go up by fourteen points. Progar was not one of the four swimmers who filed along the deck, clustered behind Chapel Gate's block.

Each of the guys in this relay would swim two lengths of a different stroke: J. T., Gaffney, Billy, Clancy; back, breast, fly, free. The two backstrokers jumped in the water as the starter, Mr. Bolt, loaded his pistol. It was always uplifting to see your high school math teacher striding along the pool deck in an ice cream vendor's uniform carrying a toy gun. The crowd quieted for his commands, which he seemed to make a point not to yell.

"Judges and timers ready."

J. T. appeared to screw first one hand and then the other into the starting block.

"Swimmers take your mark."

The two backstrokers hunched into the wall. The crack of the gun set off an avalanche of screams as the swimmers plunged back into the water and took off down the pool, stroke for sweeping stroke. Even their expressions seemed synchronized when they approached the turn and reached back meditatively for the wall. They flipped together, they swam the second length together, and they touched together while Gaffney and his opposite number hung side by side over the water. Gaffney did managed to look dogged even in midair. Nonetheless, I couldn't help but admire his long breaststroker's glide and kick; he was at his most likable underwater. The crowd caught its breath as the surface of the water grew still over the submerged swimmers. It exploded again when the breaststrokers emerged, seemingly as startled as everyone else, and gulped their way furiously to the other end of the pool. Gaffney opened up a body length lead.

Ted would never forget the fatal image that opened Billy's leg of the medley relay. He had the perfect view. Waving his towel propeller-style like the rest of his banshee teammates, he had worked his way around to the far end of the pool so that he was sighting straight along the lane lines to the starting blocks. How can one best describe the object that, before Chapel Gate's butterflyer had so much as left his block, broke the plane of the water in Billy's lane? A periscope? Not quite ominous enough. A dorsal fin, perhaps? At its appearance, a gasp went up simultaneously from both sides of the pool. But in one camp it turned into a groan and in the other into a wild, incredulous cheer.

Somehow in the frenzy all around him, my brother Billy had transported himself mentally to the end of the meet, where he was slated to swim third in the final relay as well. As he surfaced after his racing dive he started one of his looping freestyle strokes. When he stopped his hand at its apogee he seemed for a minute to be waving to the crowd. Then he reversed his stroke and began a jerky but powerful butterfly that lengthened the lead Gaffney had given him. Clancy preserved it, stroking into the wall to polite applause. Because the event was over the minute Billy broke his butterfly form. We were disqualified, and we were also dead even with Chapel Gate. They had won the medley without Progar.

Ted realized only then that the screaming person next to him had been his other brother, Chip. He ripped the towel off his head and threw it to the ground.

After the medley relays the crowd noise settled and the individual events began. The eight-and-under swimmers swam their one-length race like shipwreck survivors; they only got to the other end of the pool at all if the current was right, but their results still counted in the final score; so you found yourself in the sort of ridiculous position of standing at the side of the pool cheering for little kids. In the boys' race I watched a neighbor of ours, George Tierney, whose torso combined a potbelly and an emaciated rib cage. He would take four or five hummingbird strokes, then throw his head back despairingly for air; but he usually won, and he did that night, too.

Sometime after the thirteen and fourteen-year-olds, a sense of history settled over the crowd. It was already a classic meet. The score seesawed back and forth with every event. Everyone associated with Community felt a warm glow when Denise Matthews took the stand for her fifty. She was an imposing physical specimen, with a boy's hips and the shoulders of a stevedore. She had breasts, but they seemed kind of isolated on her broad, shallow torso, like those knobs set in the middle of fancy dining room doors. While the other girls shook out their arms and legs, Cindy stood on the far block prayerfully, clenching her hands to her chest. At the conclusion of the race, she turned like a stranded sailor scanning the horizon for a ship. The pool was calm and empty; she had finished last. Denise was first, however, and we gained another point on Chapel Gate.

At last it came time for the race everyone had come to see. Even the other swimmers turned into rank spectators. Ordinarily at these meets the times were faster the higher the age group. It was always kind of a letdown when some thirteen-year-old was the fastest swimmer of the night, and that did happen sometimes.

Not tonight. For a couple of events before his hundred free, Chip laid inert on his back on the grass, gingerly lifting a sweat-suited limb every so often and rotating it in its joint. Across the pool, Progar was stripped to his suit, still glad-handing with his teammates and friendly spectators. When they were announced, Chip and J. T. shook hands, then walked over for the ritual greeting of Progar and Whitacre, the other Chapel Gate swimmer. The timers stepped back respectfully from the blocks. Progar dove into his lane to get wet. When he muscled-up back onto the deck his black crew cut glistened like a pelt. Meanwhile, Chip knelt at the side of the pool and splashed a few handfuls of water over his chest and shoulders.

At that point the tribal chants arose from either side of the pool. Chapel Gate's was deep and steady. Hooty and I decided it was adapted from the invocation of some Norse god: "Pro-gar, Pro-gar." Ours started slow but revved: "One-two, one-two, one-two."

Mr. Bolt was known as a deliberate starter; he always made you hold your mark until he was sure everyone was steady. This time

Whitacre false started from the far block; nearest to us, J. T. fell lazily after him into the water. Chip and Progar stepped down. A second time Mr. Bolt brought them to their mark. As he coiled into position, Chip slowly brought his hands back to rest on the small of his back. Progar stretched his arms out in front of him in a muscular salaam. The gun cracked. It was a clean start.

The swimmers pulled away from the wall like a powerboat with four outboard motors, and their feet slapped the wall together at the far end. There was the sudden lull after they turned and pushed off, then their kicks churned in unison again. On the second length Whitacre started to fall back, and J. T. missed his next turn just slightly, leaving Chip and Progar side by side in the middle of the pool. That was what everyone wanted, and they yelled all the louder when they got it.

The contrast between them couldn't have been any sharper. Chip glided along as though he planned to go another mile, while Progar flailed beside him, seeming to take five or six strokes for every one of Chip's. Every time Progar breathed he seemed to be peering over the edge of a foamy trench, only to have to put his head back down in alarm and dig some more. Chip hardly seemed to turn his head for air. At the end of the race, without the slightest variation in his speed, Chip knifed his hand into the wall, and Progar took an overhand slap at it, a tenth or two of a second too late. Then he slapped the water again in frustration. J. T. finished third. We had gained another three points on them.

The Starting Block

In a way we were in the worst possible position before the last relay. A couple of our swimmers had done better than expected, so that we went into the boys' seventeen-and-over freestyle relay ahead by six points. That meant we would either win the meet by thirteen points or lose by one. In other words, we needed to win the final relay despite our lead. We might as well have been down by six points.

"Remember, this is the freestyle relay," Chip said to Billy. "Don't swim butterfly this time."

Our relay team—Clancy, Gaffney, Billy and Chip—had clustered around Ed by the pool deck.

"Actually, he could," Gaffney said. "Freestyle means that, literally, you can swim any stroke. Butterfly would be legal in the freestyle relay, but not the other way around."

"Shut your mouth, Gaffney," Ed said.

They walked in order along the deck to the start. Chapel Gate's team was bunched around Progar behind their block.

Everybody in the club that night saw it happen. Mr. Bolt spun away in embarrassment as much as disgust. Chip left the block for the anchor leg of the relay a body length ahead of Progar, and he finished a body length ahead of him. And we lost the relay and the meet. Billy had false started before Chip had even entered the pool!

I found Billy later in a chair by the baby pool. His only company was its centerpiece, a spouting concrete whale. He was to date the most miserable looking person I had ever seen. His face seemed to ache. All around us a party was in progress. Everyone from Community, including the parents, had been urged to stay and swim and eat. Chapel Gate was naturally a gracious host. They had won. Under a certain amount of duress, our team had stayed; and now everyone seemed to be having fun. Chip was the only one I knew for sure had left.

Without looking at me, Billy said, "I don't want to stay, and I don't want to go home."

I pulled up a chaise lounge but, rather than reclining, sat on the bottom edge.

"I wanted to give Chip as big a lead as possible. I wanted to make it easy for him," Billy said.

There had been nothing close or controversial about Billy's false start. Well before Gaffney touched the wall he was in midair. His only connection with solid ground was gravity.

Half an hour later, after I had done some half-hearted socializing and Hooty was ready to go, I returned to the baby pool, but Billy was gone. I was told that J. T. had fetched him, and I found him down by the woods with the reassembled relay.

CHAPTER TWENTY-ONE

The Relay After the Meet

Now, as to Teddy's alleged (admittedly, by himself) sighting of a naked Cindy Flood unnaturally early in their relationship, the experience was not as pleasant as he would have expected. Very little about the night of the first Chapel Gate meet was pleasant, during or after it.

Around nine-thirty, in shallow summer dark, my ears ringing with the chorus of crickets, I stood at the edge of Chapel Gate's parking lot, where it petered out in crumbs of asphalt into weeds and then the woods. But I didn't know why. Behind me loomed the back wall of the club. From somewhere out in front of me came the rustling of trees. J. T. was rooting around for a plank or a thick branch. I didn't know why he was doing that, either.

Leering solicitously, Scott Clancy laid a hand on Billy's

shoulder and said, "You're going to feel a lot better."

John Emley had waded thigh-deep into the weeds. Maybe he could see what was going on in the trees.

"Oh, my God, Orum," he kept saying, striking a self-conscious balance between outrage and amusement. As a blasphemer he made Hooty and me seem like a couple of amateurs. "Oh, for God's sake."

"What are you doing out here?" Hooty asked from my blind side.

Over Hooty's shoulder a streetlight gleamed from another corner of the parking lot. In the muggy dark it seemed either high up or far away or both. The only other light came from a triangle of slats high on the wall above us.

"You tell me," I said.

"I looked around, and the team was gone," he said. "I was alone in hostile territory."

"Good God," Emley said.

Just at that moment J. T. backed out of the woods dragging what looked like a fallen tree trunk.

"It doesn't need to be that big," Dillon, another of the older guys, said more matter-of-factly.

Without a word, J. T. dropped the log and turned back into the brush. I shrugged at Hooty.

"Is Chip in there?" Hooty said.

"He went home."

Hooty's pointed questions led me to ask what I was doing down here with this particular group of guys. At first I seemed to be crashing some eerie two-hour reunion of that night's relay teams. But there were also all these hangers-on. Ordinarily, J. T. wouldn't be seen socially with any of these other guys, or with me, unless Chip was present. Everyone else who was there was either on the alternate relay squad, or second man in the individual events, or just a jerk, like Emley. When Emley, for example, got to swim he would stand on the block hyperventilating and eyeballing the far wall just like the regulars; (even the biggest doggers couldn't help snapping their lats like Olympians before the start of a race); but the rest of the time Emley lounged around the pool and boasted about what bad shape he was in. For some reason guys with a gut slung their suits especially low; Emley offered a hint of cleavage from the back every time he climbed out of the pool or sat down on the deck and drew his knees up to his chest. A couple of other second-stringers stood near him. Gaffney was off by himself in his familiar knowing slouch. Despite his smirk, he didn't have any more of an idea ABOUT what was going on than I did.

J. T. emerged from the woods with what looked like a petrified two-by-four. Grinning with satisfaction, he leaned it against the wall of the club.

"That's more like it," Clancy said.

"What are you talking about? It's perfect," J.T. proclaimed.

At the edge of the woods, where he had remained, Emley

performed a little pirouette of disgust.

"You aren't actually going to do this?" he asked in awe.

"I'm not going to do anything," J. T. said. "William Livinsgstone is, for the honor of team and family, which in his case, is one and the same thing."

Clancy walked over to the wall and examined some kind of pipe that ran flush along its rough wooden surface. He followed it with his glance up twenty feet or so to the faintly lit, triangular lattice just under the peak of the roof.

"It don't look too strong," he said.

Teddy never really worried in a situation like this until the grammar started to go.

As he worked the thin end of the board between the pipe and the wall, J. T., the contented craftsman, repeated a phrase absently to himself like the refrain of a current hit song, "Oh, I hate to lose to Chapel Gate."

"Dear God in heaven," Emley exclaimed, as though trying to rekindle the embers of a dropped discussion.

"Teddy. Run look around back and see if it's clear," Clancy said.

Surprised into obedience, since I wasn't aware that Clancy knew my name, I checked around the corner of the clubhouse. There was no sign of life. The stagnant asphalt tennis courts glinted gray in the moonlight behind their fence.

J. T. eased pressure onto the board, opening up a gap between the pipe and the wall. "Billy Boy," he said. "You can do the rest." Then, as he worked his way back to the end of the two-by-four, increasing his leverage, we heard a distinct "ping."

"Oh, my God," Emley said, a note of tragedy in his voice. "You popped a bracket up above there."

"No," Clancy said, all of a sudden both decisive and candid. "It won't hold him."

"Gee, that's very disappointing," J. T. said. "Are you sure?"

There was a humid pause in the proceedings.

"I'll do it," I said.

J. T. turned toward me wordlessly, surprised but receptive.

"He's already done his part," Gaffney said.

Teddy was surprised to find support in that quarter. On the other hand, Gaffney could still be counted on to miss the single most important aspect of a given situation.

"I'm the lightest," I said.

Teddy started up the drainpipe wearing the handprint of each of his teammates on his butt. Iwo Jima-style, they had boosted him up over the board manned by J. T. If he twisted his foot, Ted could just work it between metal and wood. Eased away from the wall, the pipe was reminiscent of the rope he had had to climb in gym class; but as he looked up its length, he wasn't sure he could complete this particular drill. He understood by that time what its object was, and it wasn't to touch the ceiling.

"Maybe he'll see Progar's mother," Gaffney said.

The guy did have a certain innocence; he had probably just made for the occasion the dirtiest remark of which he was capable.

"No, she uses the men's locker room," Emley said, enjoying his first honest laugh of the evening, at his own joke.

Teddy felt a great relief when he reached the fanlight, but not just because the climb was over. For the first time that night he was alone, and he enjoyed his sudden privacy. He could get a little comfortable by resting his forearm on a sort of wooden sill in front of him and leaning into the wall. At his height, the whispered exhortations of his friends beneath him were indistinguishable from the rustling of nearby leaves. He found himself looking down into a labyrinth of empty shower stalls and a dressing area beyond which, sure enough, there were several girls in various stages of undress, including total. He was sure that his vantage point was the moral victory J. T. was after, and that he could now descend to congratulations.

But he didn't move. What held him in place was not the consideration that his position was probably more precarious, morally as well as physically, than it felt; not simple lust, but a more sincere desire for instruction than he had ever felt in any classroom. He became an instant student of the female form. He had not realized after all how much a girl's tank suit covered. After a while, the whole scene started to seem funny. To his unpracticed eye, a group of women with their clothes off seemed to be the most exotic costume party of all. It was as though female nudity was a formal affair. His enlightenment deepened when he realized that the beautiful young woman tilting her head back to catch her hair in a towel, and in the process arching her trunk toward him like that of a bent sapling, was not only nude but also Cindy. Of all the girls she somehow seemed least aware that she was naked, let alone observed.

In fact, this was Community's team, not Chapel Gate's. He had scaled the wrong drainpipe and peered in the wrong locker room.

Teddy's reverie was ruffled by a scream and a final insight. The woman he saw preparing to fling a wet towel, was not Progar's mother but his own!. He could only hope she did not recognize him through the small opening. At least she wasn't naked!

As Teddy grabbed for the pipe again with fingers suddenly itchy with fear he heard a snap. Fortunately it proved to emanate from the board far below rather than from the pipe. However, his ankle was pinned to the wall.

"Oh, Lord," Emley gasped as people below started to scatter; but he had dropped any pretense of censoriousness, and he was giggling like a little girl.

Once Ted got his foot free he tried to cling to and slide down the pipe at the same time. His speed picked up; at some point it became free fall. After some midair scrambling he landed square on his right shoulder in the parking lot. His brother Billy helped him up and half dragged him into Hooty's car, which was idling nearby. As they crested the hill out of the club's lot the first wave of outraged parents spilled out of the gate to comb the vicinity for voyeurs. Billy and Teddy sat in the back seat while Hooty drove like a chauffeur. This time Ted was just as glad Billy didn't seem to want to talk.

CHAPTER TWENTY-TWO

I Get a Private Pep Talk From My Brother

Something else happened that night. I won a race.

Teddy mentioned earlier that the performance of some of Community's swimmers exceeded all expectations. That statement applied to no one more than to himself.

As I lay on my bed at home, holding to my shoulder the pack of ice that Billy had insisted I tuck discreetly under the sleeve of my tee shirt, I felt pretty bad about the events of the evening. I still wasn't quite comfortable with my new identity as peeping tom—make that incestuous peeping tom—even if the act was well intentioned as a defense of Billy and revenge against Chapel Gate, which it probably wasn't. Billy and I had sneaked back into the house and made our movements before our parents returned as vague as possible. Chip was presumably back in his room and not to be disturbed. By scattering a few dishes around the kitchen, Billy simulated the remains of a major meal, then went over to his girlfriend's house.

After sitting up in bed for a while I felt like one of those strangely shaped objects in physics class that do not contain their own centers of gravity. The throbbing of my shoulder, while extremely painful, seemed to go on just outside my body. Meanwhile, the core of my being meditated my victory, making me as calm as a Buddha.

I was ostensibly second man for Community in the race, as always, and was hence assigned an outside rather than a middle lane. Hooty had made a career out of beating me in the fifty free, from eight-and-under on up. He had one of the more distinctive strokes on the team, skimming the water with a left arm like a scythe as he breathed and recovering normally with his right arm. Accordingly, Billy and I had nicknamed him "The Reaper," but it didn't stick; because I don't think anyone else got it. He was a strong swimmer, but he seemed to have peaked when he was about twelve. Chapel Gate's new prime young swimmers were twin brothers who had moved into the school district from California over the winter. Everyone simply assumed therefore that they were Olympic-caliber, having come from California.

Just before the race I felt a hand on my shoulder. I turned around to be wished a simple "Good luck" by Cindy. The sight of her open, though at that point largely clothed, beauty destroyed whatever vestiges of a psych had survived the screams that followed the announcement of our names over the P. A. system.

It was comforting to be on an outside block as I stood on the rim of that canyon of human faces.

Somehow as soon as I submerged I swelled, like one of those pellets that turns into a paper flower in a drinking glass. The white rush of water washed all the crowd noise off me, and after four or five strokes I saw nothing ahead of me but the wall. After I turned, I glimpsed Hooty's heels going the other way. I was a body length ahead of him any way I figured it, but on the second length I stopped figuring and started soaring. Each stroke felt better than the one before. The small of my back told me my feet were kicking in perfect time. Although I was breathing away from the other swimmers, I sensed that the water ahead of me was as empty as an ocean.

When I got out of the pool and walked backed to rejoin the team some adult member of Chapel Gate, probably the father of a swimmer, yelled, "They hid him in an outside lane" right through me, as though I couldn't hear any more than a poster could.

As I lay turning my victory over and over like an artifact in the light of my bedside lamp that night, in my more sober moments hoping that any manhunt for the voyeurs had been called off, my father's face, at its most brisk and businesslike, appeared in the doorway. I hoped he was just tired and not incensed. The terry cloth jacket he donned for pool parties made him look a little less menacing, and he was wearing that now.

"Hey, champ," he said, with a jerk of his head to one side. "Your big brother wants to talk to you."

Then he continued down the hall to his room.

One surprising aftermath of my win was that I had no one to talk to about it. In my elation I managed to remember that I hated a boastful winner almost as much as an incredulous one, one of those guys who need to be convinced that they actually came in first. Of course, before that night I just hated anyone who won. I certainly couldn't discuss my triumph in any detail with Billy after his faux pas in the medley relay, or with Hooty, whose era I had just ended, and Chip had psyching for his confrontation with Progar; and then he was gone.

And I didn't know what was on his mind now.

As I rounded his doorjamb, I found Chip in exactly the posture I had just vacated, sitting on his bed with his back up against the wall. A paperback lay open over one knee.

"Hi," I said. "Dad said you wanted to see me."

"Right," Chip said. "How was the party?"

"It was all right," I said. "Considering it was a defeat party."

I would just as soon he got the details from J. T., if at all.

"That's what I figured," Chip said as he marked his place and twisted to one side to set the book on his dresser. "There was something I wanted to talk to you about," he said. "You can sit down," he added.

I took him up on this kind offer, sitting in his armchair and reaching over with my good arm to riffle through the pages of the latest *Playboy*, although I left it flat on the table. August was traditionally almost as skimpy an issue as February.

"This is going to be difficult to explain," Chip went on, "but someone should tell you as soon as possible."

I sat back and frowned attentively.

"You won your first race tonight. That was your first win, wasn't it?"

"Yes."

"Well, winning your first race is actually a downer. It's exciting at first, I know. I remember. The problem is that from that point on people expect you to win. Winning becomes your job. People only notice if you don't do it." He stopped talking for a moment and then added, "I hope telling you this helps you to know what to expect."

Teddy left the room rather numbly, at least until he caught his shoulder on the doorjamb, but even as he walked back down the hall through a red fog of pain, he felt let off easy. He might have asked Chip what it felt like to have sex for the first time.

Fortunately, he was pretty sure Chip wouldn't know.

CHAPTER TWENTY-THREE

My Odyssey Begins

When Teddy woke up on the Monday morning following the first Chapel Gate meet, he had a sort of vision. His mission for the day appeared before his inner eye with perfect clarity. There was someplace he had to go, a place he had not been for some time.

It wasn't the pool. Ed had cancelled practice so the team could recover—me from my mysterious shoulder injury, Billy from any suicidal urges he might feel after blowing the meet. Ed had given us the standard post-meet pep talk/consolation. No one person loses a meet. It's a team sport despite the fact that it consists of individual events. If someone else had won an event, one disqualified relay wouldn't matter. He diplomatically did not point out that Billy had disqualified two relays that night. I don't think anyone believed a word of his speech, least of all Billy, who sat apart with a towel over his head, although it may have been sackcloth. He could have gotten some ashes to go with it from the barbeque pit.

Part of Teddy wanted to keep twenty-four-hour watch over Billy to protect him from harm, self-inflicted or older-brother-inflicted. Another part never wanted to be in his presence again.

The latter option was difficult when he shared a room with him. At least he didn't have to be seen in his presence.

On this Monday Teddy made a point to get up before Billy. Of course, given Billy's sleeping habits, that was no great feat. On this particular morning Billy was lying on his stomach. He seemed to be straining into the mattress, as though trying to merge with it into one solid mass of inertness. It looked like quite a concerted effort for someone who was all but comatose.

The trick was to get up before Billy, but not so early that he would run into his father as he got ready for work. Chip was long gone; his AAU team was working out as usual. Mr. Livingstone's routine involved several trips back and forth from his bedroom to the kitchen in his private atmosphere of after-shave and coffee fumes, on any one of which he might run into his son and be forced to produce some fatherly pleasantries. He might well inquire about Teddy's plans for the day. Any that Teddy had ever produced in the past had met his father's considered approval. He was pretty sure that if he had announced on a given day that he planned to enter a monastery or nationalize the steel industry his father would have nodded and wished him good luck, but he couldn't run the risk that today his father's question might be sincere.

He thought he heard the front door close and a car start—his father drove to the shopping center, where he parked and then caught the bus into town—but these sounds could constitute a ruse if his father had just gone outside to get the morning paper. However, when he stepped into the stillness of the hallway, he learned that his fears were unfounded. His father was gone. It was even conceivable that his mother had vacated the house as she obviously had left the kitchen. His mother and the neighbor, Mrs. Cross, spent part of almost every morning at either their breakfast table or Mrs. Cross' over a cup of coffee; but it was still a little early for their tête-à-tête. Under ordinary circumstances, Teddy rather enjoyed these sessions himself in his capacity as a "too young to drink coffee and appreciate adult concerns" spectator. The simple comments he did offer would be applauded as precocious. One of these mornings he might really astonish them by knocking back a cup of Hills Brothers. He liked the smell of coffee, but was nauseated by the beverage itself.

His luck did not extend that far. Just as he was preparing a surreptitious glass of vanilla instant breakfast—going so far as to stir the powder into the milk rather than fire up the blender, which would produce a superior consistency in the final product, but at the cost of telltale noise—his mother emerged from the basement with an empty laundry basket in her arms. She almost dropped it when she saw her youngest son standing at the counter.

"Good morning, Marge," I said.

Ted had found that addressing one's parent by his or her first name was a very effective way of putting them on the defensive, although to her credit Ted's mother absorbed this familiarity with a smirk.

"You gave me a turn," she said. "I didn't expect to see you up. I thought you and your brother would sleep in. I thought you didn't have practice."

"We don't," I said. "But it's never too early to turn over a new leaf in life, I always say. You see, all those workouts have instilled the virtue of early rising in me. That's the point of it, after all."

It was clear from my mother's expression that she was deciding how seriously to take me. There was just the off chance that I was forming a character.

"Teddy," she finally said, apparently I wasn't. "Are you working at the Fikes' today?"

"No," I confessed.

Not that that explanation would have worked anyway. Mom knew I never began yard work before ten, when the grass would still be dewy. I hated nothing more than clippings shooting out of a lawn mower in clumps. That necessitated a raking of the lawn afterward, a measure I avoided at all costs. Grass catchers weren't much better, since early in the summer they had to be emptied every row or two. And, although Mom and Mrs. Fike had never to my knowledge met over a cup of coffee, Mom could always drive by the Fikes' by chance and note the unattended yard.

"So, what are your plans for this glorious day?" Mom asked.

It became clear to Ted at that point that he had miscalculated. He had forgotten how truly negligible a sixteen-year-old was. He needed to offer no explanation of his movements to his mother, not even of the perfunctory variety with which he favored his father. He might simply have walked through the kitchen and out the door unobserved. He realized to his horror that his mother had not been suspicious to begin with, only startled. Now began the more difficult task of allaying misgivings he had just created. He had embarked upon a series of quasi-truths and half-truths the end of which he could not at the moment see. To this question of his mother's he was forced to respond with the day's first bold-faced lie.

"No plans," I said. "I think I'll watch some TV."

Ten minutes later his mother stuck her head in the family room.

"Have you become a Loretta Young fan?" she asked.

It was true that Ted found little inherent interest in the program he was watching. At last his mother announced, to his relief, that this was her morning to go next door to the Cross' house for coffee. Then, after a decent interval—up to the next commercial—Ted followed the televised drama. When he turned off the set, silence fell over the house. Ted eased out the front door and began his day's odyssey.

CHAPTER TWENTY-FOUR

Summer School

In school, the year before, Teddy's English class read the story about Odysseus and the oar. After ten years of wandering around the ocean, narrowly escaping its many dangers, particularly the women who seemed to hang around the seashore, luring sailors onto rocks and, if that didn't work, turning them into swine, Odysseus was just sick to death of the water. He wanted to get as far away from it as possible. He laid an oar on his shoulder and started walking inland. He decided that when he met someone who asked what that funny object was that he was carrying, he would stop and put down roots. Then he would begin his career as a landlubber.

I, myself, had now had my fill of the water—chlorinated, though, rather than salt water. Who knew how Billy felt? As I walked out into my native suburban streets, I imagined him mired in his bed like some mythical hero being punished in the underworld, stuck on a nightmarish starting block, hanging over an abyss and watching his teammate far below swimming into the wall, getting closer and closer but never quite arriving, never touching the wall to release Billy, allowing him to dive in legally.

As far as I knew we had no oar in the house, not even in the remotest corner of the attic or garage, but that's not what I needed. Setting out in that clear, bright morning I would have liked to have put a kickboard on my shoulder. When I had walked far enough into the city or out in the country so that someone asked me what that blue Styrofoam tombstone-looking thing was that I was carrying; i.e., thinking I may be a gravedigger or the like, I would know I was nowhere near a swimming pool.

By the time Teddy crossed Powers Run Road and left his neighborhood for the wider world of Fox Chapel, it was no longer all that early. The suburban adult male work force had departed; the cars left in the driveways were the station wagons, the fleet in which mothers would ferry their children to pools that were holding practice or would open their gates to all their members at noon. Judging from the clear blue sky overhead, the clubs would do a land office business; the water would seethe with thrashing bodies. Teddy's would not be one of them. He would not be gainfully employed either. Apart from his one objective, he had resolved to accomplish as close to nothing as possible that day. His momentary guilt at the thought deepened every time a truck passed full of his competition, what he thought of as industrial gardeners. These were teams of slick-skinned, dark-haired workers in white tee shirts and green trousers imported into the suburbs. The names on the doors of their trucks that often hauled trailers bristling with tools, ended in a or an o. They were headed farther out into Fox Chapel, to the big estates with lawns they would cut two mowers at a time, sometimes cross-hatching. They weren't as fastidious as Teddy about their work conditions. He had seen some of them cut grass in a near-downpour, and then clamber back into their truck and bolt for the next job.

In the absence of sidewalks, which his parents were always lamenting, Teddy tightroped the curb along Cabin Lane or walked the fringes of lawns. When he rounded the corner he came upon another place that was not his destination.

Fox Chapel High School lay sprawled in front of him like a sleeping red brick dragon. At the tip of its far wing was the gym; at the other end, closest to him, was the entrance to the auditorium. Dormant as the building was, it mesmerized him. He had escaped it barely a month before, and all his instincts beseeched him not to rouse it, not to risk being yanked back inside, thrown into the dungeon of a vacant study hall to languish until the school year started; but he couldn't resist circling it, starting up Field Club Road on the school side of the street, casting an occasional glance down at it. As always, there were a few cars parked in the lot, even on this, the most summery of days, particularly around the administrative offices. Adults he didn't recognize, men in coats and ties, entered and exited at long intervals. For that matter, they were visible during the school year, doing whatever they did—not teach. Every so often when you were driving by you might see a teacher leave the building in shorts. Teddy's impulse was to avert his eyes in embarrassment.

He had just broken the spell he was in and quickened his pace when a familiar figure, dressed in neither shorts nor a coat and tie, but in navy blue from head to foot, appeared on the sidewalk below squinting up at him. Exercising very little volition, Teddy found himself walking down the grassy bank toward the figure as though he had been hailed. He felt a little like a meteor pulled out of its orbit and falling into the mass of the school.

"How you doing?" the short, squat man said to me. He was distinctly shorter and squatter than the year before. Luckily, the more we students dwarfed him, the better he seemed to like it.

"Fine," I said, which I supposed was true. "How about you?"

"Good," he said. "Real good. What are you doing, thumbing?"

"No, just walking," I said.

"Walking?"

I had always suspected that Tony Grosso, the school's head custodian, considered himself kind of adjunct faculty, and we had embarked on a typically Socratic dialogue.

"Don't you drive yet?"

"Not yet."

"When will you?"

He liked to establish one point before moving on to the next.

"Pretty soon."

"Oh, okay," Tony said.

"I didn't expect to see you here."

"Ah, we work all summer. Got to get the place ready for you guys. How are your brothers doing?"

"Fine," I said, which may have been true on average, but to say "average" might have been misleading. "Billy's got a job, but Chip spends most of his time swimming."

"Chip graduated, you know," Tony said rather solemnly, as though he might be breaking the news to me.

"I know."

"He going to college?"

"He's going to Pitt."

"Is he?"

With that rhetorical question our conversation seemed to have run its course, but with Tony silences were never awkward. I'm not sure he even noticed them. In the midst of a school day, when classes changed, I liked to just stand next to him. He would prop his chin on the end of his broom handle and watch the students mill through the halls with a dreamy smile on his face. He seemed to accept that we all had concerns beyond his ken; he was content to get a point or two across to us. For instance, I assumed that he had mentioned my brothers for a reason.

"I guess you heard about the meet," I said.

Tony looked up at me sharply in what I took to be not an awkward but a discreet silence.

Instead of answering me, he brightened and said, "Hey."

He must have thought of a lesson plan.

"You got a minute? Come see what goes on when you're not here," he said.

Before Teddy knew it he was in the bowels of the beast, standing beside Tony not in one of the shady classrooms that lined the halls like linoleum grottoes but in the boiler room breaking up cardboard boxes. Teddy could be pretty sure no ray of sunlight had ever penetrated this space. All of a sudden summer was a myth. Around them on the floor were pallets loaded with tubs of chemicals. Their discussion was unrelated to their surroundings and activity; it had turned at some point to the advantages and drawbacks of air conditioning in cars. Tony himself was of two minds on the subject.

"I know," Tony said abruptly. "Come see."

I followed him back into the halls. By the cavern of the empty cafeteria we passed a teacher.

"Hi, Tone," he said, and nodded at me.

Although I had never had him in class, I addressed him by

name in the event that I might someday. Advance obsequiousness was never a bad policy. When we turned into the gym lobby, its windows were sudden sheets of light. Through them I could see the buses parked in the back lot that I hadn't noticed from the far side of the school. I thought I knew where we were going now. We passed the gym doors and walked to the end of the hallway.

Tony held the door open for me and beamed, as though he were hosting a party and said, "They're doing like you and your brothers do."

Teddy tried to look pleased. However, not only was the point of his day to avoid swimming, but in truth no place was quite as depressing to him as an indoor pool on a bright summer day. It could be comforting during a winter practice to look through the steamed-up, floor-length windows onto a snowy landscape, but today as he stood on the pool balcony Ted felt as though he were in a greenhouse when he could have been outside in the fresh air and real trees and flowers. Furthermore, any resemblance between the chaos he was witnessing in the water below and swimming was purely coincidental. These were kids about his age brought in maybe from a church camp in the city, where the shimmering surfaces you glimpsed between buildings turned out to be mirages—gravelly basketball courts rather than swimming pools. Some of the kids darted around the deck looking for a chink in the water between bodies that they could wedge themselves into. Without the lane lines, the water was as choppy as the English

Channel. Where they had open space to swim, their strokes were atrocious. They lobbed their hands out ahead of them and wagged their heads above the waves like dogs shaking a bone. Instead of the steady beat of kicking I was used to at practice, there was a din. At the deep end, a line formed behind the low dive. The kids approached it in visible awe, as though the springboard tapped some mystical source of power. No three-step approaches for them. They would start at the end of the board, sprint its length and jump with all their might at the end to launch themselves into the void. As often as not they would describe a slow, three-quarter somersault in the air and land square on their backs with a slap of water. For the divers the pool was more like the River Lethe, since they seemed to forget each near-fatal belly flop and get right back in line with beet red shoulder blades.

We stood there for a while unobserved and in silence. For Tony the scene was self-explanatory. I was surprised at my reaction. I was happy to stand there and watch. At first I had been disgusted at the display of amateur swimming by my contemporaries. Then I realized that I envied their innocence. These kids weren't doing endless laps; they weren't timing each other. No one in that pool was losing.

At last I sensed Tony grow more serious. I assumed he had to get back to work. It turned out that he was worried about my schedule.

"I don't want to keep you," he said. "You don't want to keep the guy waiting, you know what I mean?"

The Starting Block

"What guy?" I asked.

"Whoever it is you're meeting."

My expression remained blank.

"You asked me if I knew about 'the meet.'"

"Not *that* kind of meet, Tony."

"Oh," he said. "Okay."

CHAPTER TWENTY-FIVE

The Ride

As Teddy labored up the far driveway from the school back to Field Club Road, he reflected that he might already be able to lay down his kickboard and call an end to his quest. He had discovered a place so remote from his reality that its inhabitants had not heard of swim meets, much less his team's defeat and his brother's disgrace. Ironically, that place was a swimming pool.

My head down, trudging along, I realized that I was not only a little tired, but also a little warm. The sky was still blue, but not quite as clear as before, frosted over with heat that would settle over the afternoon. When I raised my gaze to the road, I was confused: a car was pulled over onto the shoulder, as though waiting for me. I approached it a little warily, walking around it on the passenger's side, peering in as casually as I could. I was almost past it before I recognized the driver. My classmate Donnie Uehling sat behind the steering wheel grinning out at me. The car was waiting for me.

"Yins want a ride?" he asked. "I seen you walking up the hill."

I had intended to walk on my odyssey that day as a mild penance, but the habit had become deeply ingrained in me over the years never to turn down a ride, regardless of its direction.

"Thanks," I said.

"Yins going to the shopping center?" he asked with a sudden urgency as I got in.

Donnie was one of the few speakers of Pittsburgh dialect who addressed individuals with "yins"; ordinarily the word was plural. He was a little old for our class, so he got his license early and had been driving more or less continuously ever since. In whatever corner of the township you found yourself, you could pretty much count on seeing Donnie pass on the road, often with newly acquired friends as his passengers. I might be Odysseus for a day, but he was the Flying Dutchman in a Ford Fairlane. I had never been in the vehicle before this. It must have been his father's car: the seats were covered with plastic, and there was a tang of cigar smoke in the air. I had never known Donnie to light up a stogie.

I had naturally assumed when Donnie offered me a ride to the shopping center, that it was straight to where he was going. He would, in fact, be taking me past my original destination, but I could always backtrack; and the shopping center held undeniable attractions. I even had a few dollars on me, but Donnie wasn't actually going to the shopping center right away.

"You mind if we stop by the golf club?" he asked.

"No," I said. "I'm not on a schedule."

That was true enough. It was highly unlikely that Donnie's family belonged to the club, but I asked anyway.

"Do you belong to the club?"

"No," Donnie said.

I didn't have to worry that he would be deflated by my question. On the contrary, he seemed pleased by it.

"I don't have to belong. I caddy," he said.

"I didn't know that."

"Oh, yeah, " he said as he smiled and settled back in his seat with the air of a man who had it made. "It's not even like a job. We get paid to walk around the golf course."

"Sounds great."

"Yeah, but that's not the best part about it. The pay's not that good, but we get tips. And, see, to play on the course you have to have a caddy. Sometimes I go out twice a day. But that's not the best part about it."

"What's the best part?"

"The best part is that we get to play on Mondays! I'm playing today!"

I turned and saw a canvas bag of clubs lying on the back seat. I wondered for a minute if Donnie had picked me up to caddy for him, but he laid that thought to rest.

"I'm playing later on," he said. "They asked me to run an errand for them first. I'm getting paid for it. And I get mileage. I'll be back in a minute."

By that time we had pulled into the parking lot of the Fox Chapel Golf Club. I sat in the car and waited while Donnie strolled over to reception. I knew this club had both tennis courts and a swimming pool, but I wasn't sure which was which; both were surrounded by high, thick hedges. From the car, though, I could distinguish their sounds. The pop of balls on rackets came from right in front of me; to my right I heard the shrill screams of kids in the water. They had a team, too, but we didn't swim them. It was clear from the noise they weren't working out at the moment.

I hadn't noticed that a man in a green blazer and white golf shirt had approached the car.

"Excuse me," he said. "Are you a caddy?"

"No," I said.

"Lifeguard?"

"No."

Though he seemed to have exhausted all available options, he didn't seem completely satisfied, but he went back inside. While I watched him out my window Donnie got in the car and back behind the wheel.

"One more stop," he said. "Mind?"

"I've got all day," I answered.

"Yeah, you can't beat golf," Donnie said when we were back out on Fox Chapel Road.

The scent of watered grass streamed in the open windows of the car. We passed a private school and not long after the borough building; set back on sweeping lawns, the houses in between weren't much smaller. On a day like today the whole suburb smelled like a golf course. Donnie's mood remained expansive. He had the dress of a professional golfer and the grammar of a construction worker. Despite his yellow slacks and green golf shirt with the FCGC logo, which I had just noticed when he got back in the car, I had a hard time picturing him on the links. He also had the build of a construction worker. His shirt stretched tight across his stomach. Either one of my brothers, long and lean, would have made a more likely golfer.

"You play?" he asked.

"No, my family belongs to a swimming club. Just a pool. And a shuffleboard court. I swim on the team there."

"I don't like swimming," Donnie said. "No offense. You get too wet."

Since I decided to concede that point, we drove for a few minutes in silence.

"I take it back," Donnie said. "I'll get wet to find golf balls. We get to keep the balls we fish out of the water hazards., or we can sell them to the club, and they sell them back to the same guys that lost them in the first place for practice balls. It's a racket. We wear these diving goggles when we go in. I admit it feels pretty good on a hot day. Hey. Got to get some gas."

When we pulled into the Amoco station a guy who was obviously exactly our age, but whom we didn't know, came out to wait on us.

"Fill it up," Donnie said, digging a wad of bills out of his pocket. "It takes hi-test," he added, as much to me as to the attendant.

I might have thought the gas station was the extra stop on our circuit, but that turned out to be a public golf course on the other side of the Allegheny River. We drove through Oakmont, a different municipality altogether, and up the hill past Oakmont Country Club. Donnie turned left into the gravel parking lot of what no one would mistake for a country club. The only structure was the office, a small white frame house with a snack bar on the porch. Compared to the golfers here Donnie looked like a member of the PGA tour. Their standard attire was tee shirt and cut-off jeans, and they carried their own bags or pulled handcarts behind them. One guy drove off the first tee with a cigarette in his mouth. Here, again, Donnie made a trip into the office and back.

"This isn't bad for a public course," he said on his return. "You should see number ten. The green's so far down you can't even see it from the tee. It's behind a hill. You have to drive blind. So, when you swim, you have races and that?"

"We call them meets," I said. "As a matter of fact we had one a couple of days ago."

"But you race other guys."

"Yes."

"See, what I like about golf is it's you against the course. You can play another guy. You can even bet, or play hole by hole. But you end up with a score. You can't get around that. You know it, even if no one else does."

"Swimming's a little like that," I objected, even though it was my practice when hitchhiking to subscribe to whatever views on whatever subject my driver held. "The courses are all the same, almost all twenty-five yards or fifty meters; but there's always the clock. You're racing against three other guys, but also against time. And in a meet you're racing as an individual, but the whole team wins or loses." I was going to stop before I sounded too much like Ed Gow, but then I added, "Especially when it comes to relays. There you're a team of four guys."

"That's true," Donnie said.

From that point on the ride was rather businesslike. We lapsed into a comfortable silence as Donnie drove me back through Oakmont, across the Hulton Bridge and toward the shopping center. I might occasionally turn sharply to look at something out the window in lieu of a remark. I thanked him when he pulled over to drop me off. I had the feeling our decision that a handshake was not in order was mutual.

CHAPTER TWENTY-SIX

Not Quite the Last Stop

The gratitude I expressed to Donnie was genuine. The fact that the five-minute ride from the high school to the shopping center had taken an hour and fifteen minutes left me untroubled. From my perspective, this day existed to be wasted. Still, once I decided that the shopping center would be my penultimate stop, I could relax and enjoy it. In my beatitude, I could imagine that I was seeing it for the first time, or the last. Donnie had let me out on Freeport Road, the main drag through the old mill towns turned suburbs along the Allegheny River. I decided to take a closer look at that body of water, crossing the street to the far side, away from the shops, and cutting through the parking lot of a bar and grill to Old Freeport Road, that much closer to the river. I didn't get down here often, but I knew there was a marina nearby. Its gates were wide open, so I stood by the entrance and looked down the driveway, which became a launch and ran right into the water downstream of the bridge I had crossed earlier.

As I looked out on the level of the river, olive green and grooved with the wakes of barges and power boats, I realized that a couple of the men inside the marina were returning my gaze kindly, as though inviting me to step down to the water and cast off. There was a fair amount of activity in the yard, as mostly older men went back and forth between the small office to my left and several low sheds. Presumably if I waited long enough I would see a boat emerge from one of them. Maybe by that time they were all out on the river. Despite the welcoming expressions of the workers, I doubted we were kindred spirits. The water meant something different to us. They wanted to stay on top of it; I liked to be in it. Just then a couple of water skiers passed by on the river. They seemed to me an alien species with interesting but incomprehensible behavior. I liked to go fast in the water, too, but I liked to generate my own horsepower.

Teddy walked back up to Fox Chapel Road to experience what he would have to call an event on this supposedly uneventful day. He watched his family's car being stolen.

I had forgotten that my father preceded me to the shopping center that day, when he parked our car and took the bus downtown. The stores allowed commuters to park at the far fringes of the lot. Our car was always in pretty much the same place, and when I located it I saw a figure stooping furtively by the driver's side to unlock the door. It was not my father; it had hair.

Confronted with this rather dramatic development, Ted debated his course of action. That was probably a bad sign in itself. Perhaps he should instinctively have run across the street, dodging traffic, and tackled the thief. He should already be running. Before he could bring himself to move, however, the perpetrator stood up to open the door, and Teddy recognized him. It was not his father. It was his brother. For a second he wasn't sure which one.

If Chip or Billy could get themselves down to the shopping center, they were allowed to use the car, provided it was back in a nearby space when the 1A New Kensington dropped Dad off at 5:40. Often they would just wait for Dad and drive him home.

But Teddy's relief was only momentary, his decision only postponed. For when he realized it was Billy, though he no longer had to make a citizen's arrest, he still wasn't sure how to react. He wondered if he would know better if it were Chip across the street from him. Billy looked around—it was probably hard not to feel guilty even if it was your own car you were breaking into—but he didn't see Teddy, who stood rooted to the spot on the far bank of the river of traffic on Freeport Road. Even if he had yelled, his brother might not have heard him. Instead, he watched him get in the car, back out and drive away. Only then did it occur to Teddy that he might have given him a ride.

The Starting Block

Walking up and down the sidewalks of the shopping center was a little like swimming laps in a pool: once you got to the end, there wasn't much else to do but start back the other way. The foot traffic was less like a practice than free swim; Teddy weaved his way among the other shoppers, mostly housewives at this time of the day, on his way past the storefronts with a milkshake in his hand. By now, on what had been vacant fields just a few years before, in Teddy's boyhood, there were two modest strip malls on either side of Fox Chapel Road. They were pretty much identical, each with a supermarket and several specialty stores. Although the warmth outside was detrimental to the consistency of his shake, it had been too cold in the dairy store where he purchased it to drink it there. For its customers the management went beyond air conditioning to provide refrigeration. Furthermore, the drink allowed him to be noncommittal, nursing it as he looked through the display windows of the stores without going inside of them. He could easily have killed the rest of the afternoon in the hobby shop, where he would have encountered acquaintances at least as intimate as Donnie Uehling racing their miniature cars around the track, but he felt a sudden surge of purpose. He drained the waxy dregs of the milkshake, threw away the cup, walked out onto Fox Chapel Road and stuck out his thumb.

It was a risky decision. His destination was a scant mile away, though uphill, with two major turnoffs in between. Should Teddy learn a driver was going to take one of them, he would have either to decline the ride—an awkward situation for both parties—or accept a short ride and then face the same dilemma all over again when he was let out a half-mile downhill from his goal. It was beneath him to suggest that a driver alter his route.

When the third car along pulled over, his worst fears were realized and then exceeded. First of all, the car contained two females, an unlikely source of a ride. It stopped some distance beyond him, as though there might have been some hesitation on the driver's part or some debate between the passengers. Ted jogged after it, prepared to be mannerly, fawning if necessary. One of the women in the front seat was Cindy. By the time she introduced him to her mother, who had heard so much about him, but probably not that he bummed rides, they were taking the first turnoff, Delafield Road, and he was getting out of the car. He thanked Mrs. Flood. Cindy apologized to him. As he watched their station wagon drive away up the hill Teddy wondered what sort of milestone that two-minute ride marked in their relationship.

I couldn't be much more compromised than I already was, so I cocked my thumb again. This time no one so much as slowed down, but when I turned around to walk I understood why. Just as earlier in the day at the high school, there was a car pulled over waiting for me. It was a familiar car. It was a stolen car. It was our car. Billy was at the wheel.

"How did you get here?" I said as I got in.

The Starting Block

"I saw you get out of that other car when I drove by Delafield Road."

"That was Cindy and Mrs. Flood. They picked me up down by the shopping center."

I hadn't been in the car alone with Billy since our bowling night. Since the Chapel Gate meet we had been a little formal with each other, so this ride felt like a double date without the dates. On the whole it was more enjoyable than my previous ride, a double date with a girl and her mother.

"I saw you take the car from the shopping center. I was across the street. I thought you'd be long gone by now."

"I had to buy something at the store for Debbie. I'm going to take it by her house. I can take you home first."

"Thanks, but I'll get out up here."

"Or the pool, if you want?"

"Maybe later. You can pull in the lot."

"You mean this is where you're going?"

"Yes."

"It's Monday."

"I know," I said.

"Wouldn't it be closed on Monday?"

"I don't think it closes, exactly."

"Do you want me to wait for you?"

"No, thanks. I can walk the rest of the way home if I have to."

The Starting Block

As I got out of the car, it seemed that Chip should be waiting for me in another car, but the parking lot was empty save for a few vehicles over by the curb. If this was the brother relay, I had false started by a mile.

CHAPTER TWENTY-SEVEN
Monday School

It wasn't as though I couldn't turn around and walk back out. The lobby was cool, but I didn't know if it was air conditioning or a permanent chill radiated by the stone floor or all the glass. The entrance was a kind of colonnade, with a courtyard on the other side of the high windows directly across from the front door. The hallway radiated emptiness along with the cold. It wasn't obvious which way you would turn if you wanted to find another human being, but I knew the office was to the left. I walked into it and found a gray-haired woman with a pleasantly blank expression sitting at a desk. She asked if she could help me.

Before I could answer, a youthful man charged out of an inner office and stopped short melodramatically.

"Excuse me for turning white, Dorothy," he said to the woman at the desk. "I thought I saw a ghost. And not too holy a one, either."

It wasn't that pastors and parents weren't that funny that bothered Teddy. It was that they felt they ought to be funny.

The secretary relaxed a little at this outburst without quite smiling. Reverend Burns laughed for both of us.

"Where have you all been?" he asked, looking at his watch. "It's half past July. I haven't seen your family since forever. I didn't think you went away for the summer."

"I'm sure we'll be back."

"Looks like you came back early."

"I was passing by."

"Come with me," Reverend Burns said. "We'll walk and talk," he said as he led me down the hallway away from the entrance. "I've tried to explain to people that I can only do so many things, but I don't think the message has gotten through. I hope my sermons work better," he added as he pulled a cluster of keys out of his pocket. "We have a family dinner this Wednesday night, and I wonder who is going to set up the chairs?" he asked as he gave me a hard look. "Yes, I wonder," he said, and after a pause he laughed again.

It wasn't always easy to tell whether he was laughing at the joke he had just told or at the one he was about to tell.

"Say, the Livingstones are a family. They could come to the dinner," he said with a smile adding to the one-sided dialog.

"We might have a meet that night."

"A meet?" he asked.

"A swimming meet."

"I see," Reverend Burns said skeptically.

Teddy was pretty sure they wouldn't end up in the boiler room, but the dining hall, a low-ceilinged room in the basement set up with rows of long tables, was pretty close. There wasn't really all that much to do, just arrange the head table with a few folding chairs and a podium; and Teddy helped Reverend Burns move them around.

"Okay, we're done walking," he said. "Now we can start talking. Have a seat. How about something to drink?"

He went into the kitchen and came back with a couple of cold cans of Coke.

"Where have you been hiding these?" I asked. "I thought it was against our religion to serve kids any beverage other than lukewarm pineapple juice."

To his credit, Reverend Burns laughed at other people's jokes, as well as his own.

"Something tells me there's something you want to want to talk about," he said smiling; and I found that I liked his smile better than his laugh.

"I have two questions," I said.

"Shoot. You know my motto as a pastor. You've got questions, I've got more questions."

The Starting Block

"I've been going to church all my life—until recently, anyway—and I believe what I hear. I believe God will forgive me if I repent, but what if I do nothing but repent? I try to be good and to do the right thing, at least when the opportunity presents itself. To be honest, I think most of the time it doesn't matter much what I do. I'm not significant enough. I don't think what I do usually has that much effect on anything or anybody. The thing is, I spend half of that most of the time wondering if I could ever really love somebody—rather than actually doing it—and the other half trying to picture what girls would look like without their clothes on, girls I know. How could I be so hypocritical?"

"You're a teenager," Reverend Burns said. "Next question."

"Not just me. How could any human brain function that way? Or malfunction that way?"

"Next question."

"Well, last year in English class we learned about a character named Guido da Montefeltro in an old poem called *The Divine Comedy*."

Reverend Burns laughed and asked rhetorically with surprise, "You're reading Dante in tenth grade? That's rather precocious. In the original Italian?"

"We didn't actually read it. Our teacher told us the story. It related to something else we were reading. I forget what. It was in Mr. Tichon's class. I like him. I get the feeling he reads more than just the same homework we do."

"Bless his heart. You need teachers who are still students."

"Do you remember that character?"

Reverend Burns winced. "Refresh my memory."

"He ended up in hell because he wanted to be forgiven for a sin before he committed it."

"That guy," Reverend Burns said. "You have to admire his ingenuity. What a great idea! Then you could relax and enjoy the sin. Doesn't work, though. Were you thinking of trying that? Confess first, sin afterward?"

"First of all, we don't do confession, do we?" I asked.

"Not in a booth, maybe. But think back to our Sunday worship services. We always have a collective confession of sin, and we seem to need it again the next week."

"I wasn't considering that, more of a variation on it. It's part of my bigger problem. I'm trying to figure out how to love my brothers, if not in the same way, then in the same amount. I have two brothers, you know."

"Let's see. It's been a while, and you know my memory is going. Was one of them named Guido?"

This time I laughed.

"It's easier in one case than the other," I went on. "Billy has a way of messing up. He's older than I, but sometimes he seems younger. He's my younger older brother. He let our swimming team down pretty badly at this last meet we had, and I'm afraid he's going to do it again next time, in some way I can't foresee. I'm not trying to be forgiven in advance for anything. I'm wondering if I can forgive my brother in advance."

"No answers, two comments," Reverend Burns said. "First, I didn't mean to make light of your worries about sex, but the particular mental activity you described is normal for teenagers; and it doesn't stop when you hit twenty. Don't ask me how I know that. Just from hearing the concern in your voice I don't think you've hurt anyone, and I don't think you would. About your brothers? When someone loves another person deeply, I sometimes wonder who has to be forgiven. Do we need to be forgiven for loving too much, or for being too lovable? Idols come in many shapes and sizes. And if you're worried about forgiving someone for their future sins, does that mean you haven't forgiven them yet for the past?"

We sat for another minute.

"Thank you," I said, and stood up, scraping the metal folding chair back against the linoleum.

"What's your rush?" Reverend Burns asked with a smile.

It might have occurred to Teddy that they would pray.

www.ingramcontent.com/pod-product-compliance
Ingram Content Group UK Ltd.
Pitfield, Milton Keynes, MK11 3LW, UK
UKHW041953230426
12048UKWH00008B/305